THE SEAT OF
THE SCORNFUL

THE SEAT OF
THE SCORNFUL

A DEVON MYSTERY

JOHN DICKSON CARR

With an Introduction by
Martin Edwards

Poisoned Pen
PRESS

Introduction © 2022, 2023 by Martin Edwards
The Seat of the Scornful © 1942 by The Estate of Clarice M. Carr
Cover and internal design © 2023 by Sourcebooks
Cover illustration © NRM/Pictorial Collection/Science & Society Picture Library

Published by Poisoned Pen Press, an imprint of Sourcebooks,
in association with the British Library
P.O. Box 4410, Naperville, Illinois 60567-4410
(630) 961-3900
sourcebooks.com

The Seat of the Scornful was originally published in the
UK in 1942 by Hamish Hamilton, London.

Library of Congress Cataloging-in-Publication Data

Names: Carr, John Dickson, author. | Edwards, Martin,
    writer of introduction.
Title: The seat of the scornful / John Dickson Carr ; with an introduction
    by Martin Edwards.
Description: Naperville, Illinois : Poisoned Pen Press, [2023] | Series:
    British Library crime classics | The Seat of the Scornful was originally
    published in the UK in 1942 by Hamish Hamilton, London.
Identifiers: LCCN 2022052221 (print) | LCCN 2022052222
    (ebook) | (trade paperback) | (epub)
Subjects: LCGFT: Detective and mystery fiction. | Novels.
Classification: LCC PS3505.A763 S43 2023 (print) | LCC PS3505.A763
    (ebook) | DDC 813/.52--dc23/eng/20221028
LC record available at https://lccn.loc.gov/2022052221
LC ebook record available at https://lccn.loc.gov/2022052222

Printed and bound in the United States of America.
VP 10 9 8 7 6 5 4 3 2 1

INTRODUCTION

The Seat of the Scornful was first published in Britain in April 1942, having appeared in the U.S. five months earlier under the title *Death Turns the Tables*. The novel features John Dickson Carr's great detective, Dr. Gideon Fell, but I should say at the outset that for once Fell is not called upon to fathom a locked room mystery or some other form of impossible crime. This is a story in which Carr combines a pleasing mystery puzzle with an exploration of the nature of justice.

Despite Gideon Fell's exuberant presence, Carr's principal focus is on one of Fell's innumerable acquaintances; a tough-minded judge, Mr. Justice Ireton. We see the judge in court, meting out his brand of justice in a manner that borders on the sadistic. Fell plays chess with him (and there is a touch of symbolism in the chess game) but is defeated by the judge, who is as clever as he is formidable.

The judge is a widower, with a pretty but headstrong daughter aged twenty-one and called Constance. A controlling man, he wants her to marry an affable barrister called

Fred Barlow. However, Constance has fallen for a man by the name of Tony Morell, who appears to be a shady customer. When the judge learns that the couple are due to marry, he is far from happy. Soon he has reason to believe that Morell is nothing more than a gold-digger. He tries to buy off Morell, with apparent success, but then the surprises begin…

Douglas G. Greene has expressed his admiration for the novel's ingenious touches in his definitive biography, *John Dickson Carr: The Man Who Explained Miracles*. Greene explains that *The Seat of the Scornful* was Carr's own choice for the title. His American publishers, Harrap, felt that was insufficiently mysterious and chose to call it *Death Turns the Tables*, but as Greene says, this "does describe a part of the book but misses Carr's theme." So, for this edition we have retained Carr's preferred title.

Greene makes the point that, in his judicial role, Ireton "has never found weakness an excuse, or motive a justification, for committing a crime" and regards circumstantial evidence as potentially enough to prove criminal guilt. He has no time for "relationships based on mere feeling." Before long, these attitudes come under the spotlight. A corpse is discovered, and the judge is at the scene, brandishing a revolver. It appears to be an open and shut case, but Carr knows better than to make things too easy for his readers and the case quickly becomes complicated. Is it a form of "inverted mystery"—as with R. Austin Freeman's stories in *The Singing Bone*, or in Levinson and Link's *Columbo* stories for television—focusing on a detective's quest to prove a culprit guilty of an apparently perfect crime? Or is something else going on?

Greene has questioned the ethics of the final scene, and in recent years a number of bloggers have debated Carr's approach to the moral issues raised by his storyline. In this introduction, I am keen to avoid significant spoilers, but I can say that this is a novel in which Carr's ability to draw interesting and believable characters is to the fore. Perhaps the storyline reflects the fact that Carr—like his friends Agatha Christie and Anthony Berkeley—was preoccupied during the latter stages of the Golden Age of detective fiction with the profound question of whether murder can ever be justified.

I first came across *The Seat of the Scornful* as a teenager when it appeared in Hamish Hamilton's excellent "Fingerprint" reprint series, but since then copies have been hard to find. This is a pity, because as Jim Noy has said on his blog, The Invisible Event, the story's "restrained execution and structure are so brilliantly without flaw that the more easily you dismiss it the more you're falling into the very trap it lays."

John Dickson Carr (1906–77) was an American who fell in love with England (and an Englishwoman, Clarice, whom he married in 1932 without letting his parents know) and spent much of his life in Britain. Although his early crime novels featuring Henri Bencolin were set in Paris, most of his major novels have an English background and he created no fewer than three memorable detective characters in Fell, Sir Henry Merrivale, and Colonel March—who were all Englishmen. Carr was elected to the Detection Club in 1936, and soon became its Secretary; his sociable nature earned him the friendship of such diverse individuals as Christie, Berkeley, Dorothy L. Sayers, Val Gielgud, and Edmund Crispin.

Carr is best known as a novelist, but he also wrote many

entertaining short stories, as well as enjoying considerable success as an author of radio plays. His lifelong interest in "true crime" was reflected in his study of a famous case dating back to 1678, *The Murder of Sir Edmund Godfrey*. An enthusiastic Sherlockian, he produced an important biography of Sir Arthur Conan Doyle as well as collaborating with Sir Arthur's son Adrian on a book of pastiches, *The Exploits of Sherlock Holmes*.

This novel has long been out of print, perhaps because it lacks a locked room puzzle, but even though Carr was the supreme exponent of impossible crime mysteries, *The Seat of the Scornful* illustrates that there was more to him as a storyteller than that.

—Martin Edwards
www.martinedwardsbooks.com

A NOTE FROM THE PUBLISHER

The original novels and short stories reprinted in the British Library Crime Classics series were written and published in a period ranging, for the most part, from the 1890s to the 1960s. There are many elements of these stories which continue to entertain modern readers; however, in some cases there are also uses of language, instances of stereotyping, and some attitudes expressed by narrators or characters which may not be endorsed by the publishing standards of today. We acknowledge that some elements in the works selected for reprinting may make uncomfortable reading for some of our audience. With this series British Library Publishing and Poisoned Pen Press aim to offer a new readership a chance to read some of the rare books of the British Library's collections in an affordable paperback format, to enjoy their merits and to look back into the world of the twentieth century as portrayed by its writers. It is not possible to separate these stories from the history of their writing and as such the following novel is presented as it was originally published with the inclusion of minor edits made for consistency of style and sense, and with pejorative terms of an extremely offensive nature partly obscured. We welcome feedback from our readers.

CHAPTER I

"Members of the jury, have you agreed upon a verdict?"

"We have."

"Do you find the prisoner, John Edward Lypiatt, guilty or not guilty of murder?"

"Guilty."

"You say that he is guilty, and that is the verdict of you all?"

"It is. With," the foreman added, gulping hastily, "a strong recommendation to mercy."

The courtroom stirred. There had been a faint gasp at the verdict, followed by dead silence: the recommendation was too thin and slender for a cheer. Yet the wretch in the dock did not seem to think so. For the first time in that trial, an edge of hope appeared in his face. His numb eyes looked at the jury, as though he expected them to say something else.

The Clerk of Arraigns made a note of the recommendation, and cleared his throat.

"John Edward Lypiatt, you have pleaded not guilty to

murder, and put yourself upon your country. That country has now found you guilty. Have you anything to say why sentence of death should not be pronounced on you according to the law?"

The prisoner stared back dully, as though startled. He opened and shut his mouth.

The Clerk of Arraigns waited.

"I done wrong," said the prisoner humbly. "I know I done wrong."

Then a frenzied look appeared in the smeared eyes.

"But you, sir," he appealed to the judge. "And you, sir," he appealed to the Clerk of Arraigns: who, either out of stoicism or embarrassment, looked away. "I done it because I loved her. That's what I've been trying to tell you. When I come home and seen that fellow'd been there, and she laughed and admitted it, I just couldn't stand it."

He swallowed hard.

"I hit her. I know I hit her. I don't rightly know *what* I done. And then there she was lying on the floor, and the kettle boiling on the fire as though nothing had happened. But I didn't mean to do it. I *loved* her."

Not a muscle moved in Mr. Justice Ireton's face.

"Is that all you have to say?" asked the judge.

"Yes, sir."

Mr. Justice Ireton removed his spectacles, slowly disengaging them from one ear under his tie-wig, and folded them up. He put them carefully on the desk in front of him. Then he interlaced his small plump fingers, without removing those placid but terrifying eyes from the prisoner.

He was a small man, plump rather than fat. Nobody would

have guessed that under his wig he had thin ginger hair parted in the middle; or that his fingers were cramped to agony with note-taking; or that under his red robe, slashed with black, he was hot and weary at the end of the Westshire spring assizes. His clerk approached from one side, carrying the square of black silk that represented the black cap, and draped it point downward over his wig. The chaplain stood up on the other side.

Mr. Justice Ireton's voice was soft, but as detached and impersonal as death or fate.

"John Edward Lypiatt," he said, "the jury have found you guilty of the brutal murder of your wife."

He drew the air through his nostrils, slowly.

"In an attempt to justify yourself, you have pleaded that you acted in an uncontrollable fit of passion. That is no concern of ours. The law recognizes no mitigation there, except under such circumstances as you acknowledge were not present in your case. I cannot see, any more than the jury, that your counsel's plea for a verdict of manslaughter was for a moment valid."

He paused, during a bursting hush.

Counsel for the defence—Mr. Frederick Barlow, KC—sat motionless, his head down, and twiddled with a pencil. In counsel's benches behind, one of his fellow silks looked at another, and significantly turned down his thumb.

"The fact remains that, in your right senses and knowing what you were doing, you beat your wife to death. The jury have recommended you to mercy. That recommendation will be considered in the proper quarter. But I must warn you not to expect too much from it.

"There remains only for me to pass upon you the sentence

prescribed by law, which is: that you be taken hence to the place whence you came, and thence to the place of execution, there to be hanged by the neck until you are dead. And may God have mercy upon your soul."

"Amen," said the chaplain.

The befuddled look had not left the prisoner's eyes. Suddenly he seemed to go frantic.

"It ain't true!" he said. "I never meant to hurt her! I never did! Oh, my God, I wouldn't have hurt Polly!"

Mr. Justice Ireton looked at him steadily.

"You're guilty and you know it," he said flatly. "Remove the prisoner."

At the back of the small and overcrowded assize-court, a girl in a light summer dress got up from among the spectators, and began to edge her way out. She felt that she could not stand the smell of the place any longer. She tripped over large boots; she felt the heavy breathing of fascinated but uncomfortable spectators.

Her companion, a thick-set, much too well-dressed young man, first looked puzzled and then followed her. An empty bag of crisps, which somebody had discarded, crunched under her foot. Before she reached the glass doors leading out into the hall of the sessions-house, Miss Constance Ireton heard a stream of whispered comments.

"'Ardly seems 'uman, do 'e?" whispered a voice.

"Who?"

"The judge."

"Him?" said a woman's voice, with satisfaction. "*He* knows a thing or two, *he* does. He can see straight through 'em! And if they're guilty—well!"

"Ah," said the first voice, conceding the point and closing the discussion, "there's got to be law."

The hall outside was crowded. Constance Ireton went down a short passage, and out into a little garden tucked between the grey stone back of the sessions-house on one side and the grey stone back of a church on the other. Though it was only the end of April, spring with the warmth of summer kindled the clouds over the little West Country town.

Constance Ireton sat down on a bench in the centre of the garden, near a chipped and blackened stone statue of a man in a periwig. Constance was just twenty-one. She was a pretty and fresh-coloured blonde, who affected a desperately sophisticated style of makeup and hairdressing. But she could not, except among her friends in London, affect the same desperately sophisticated style of speech. Her eyes—a surprising brown, with dark eyebrows, against the fair skin and fair hair—wandered round the garden.

"I used to play here," she said, "when I was a little girl."

Her companion ignored this.

"So that's your father," he observed, jerking his head towards the sessions-house.

"Yes."

"Bit of a tough egg, isn't he?"

"No, he isn't," said the girl rather sharply. "That is—oh, I don't know what he's like, really! I never did."

"Touchy?"

"Yes, sometimes. But I never knew him to lose his temper. I doubt if he could. He never says very much. And...I say, Tony."

"Yes?"

"We've made a mistake," said Constance scuffling the toe of her slipper round in the gravel path, and studying it. "We can't possibly see him today. I forgot that this was the last day of assizes. There are all sorts of ceremonies and processions and things; and he has a traditional drink with his clerk, and—and—anyway, we *can't*. We'd better go back to Jane's party. Then tomorrow we can go to The Dunes and see him."

Her companion smiled slightly. "Not keen on facing the music, my darling?"

He stretched out his hand and walked his fingers along her shoulder. He was one of those self-consciously virile types which are associated with the Southern European; the sort of man who, as Jane Tennant once put it, always makes a woman feel that he is breathing down the back of her neck.

If he had not borne the English name of Anthony Morell, you would have taken him for an Italian. He had an olive complexion, very strong white teeth, prominent moving eyes under strongly furred eyebrows, and heavy hair which reflected back the sun. His smile was charming, and his manners languid. It was also a self-consciously intellectual face, but with a good deal of tenacity in it as well.

"Not keen on facing the music?" he repeated.

"It's not that!"

"Sure, my darling?"

"Don't you see? Today he's simply surrounded by people! But tomorrow he's going down to that bungalow he's just bought at Horseshoe Bay. There won't be anybody else there except the woman who 'does' for him. Wouldn't that be a much better time to approach him?"

"I'm beginning to think," said Mr. Morell, "that you don't love me."

Her face lit up. "Oh, Tony you know that's not true!"

Mr. Morell took her hands. "I love *you*," he said. It was impossible to doubt the raw sincerity of his manner. He was so earnest that he almost snorted. "I want to kiss your hands and your eyes and your throat and your mouth. I could go down on my knees to you, here and now."

"Tony, don't!—for heaven's sake!—no…!"

Constance would not have believed that she could have felt so powerfully embarrassed.

In London, in Chelsea, or Bloomsbury, this had seemed all right. Here, in the little garden behind the sessions-house, it seemed almost grotesque. It was as though a large dog had put its paws on her shoulders and begun to lick her face. She loved Tony Morell; but she felt obscurely that there was a time and a place for everything. And Morell, with his quick intuition, saw it. He sat back, smiling slightly.

"More repressions, my darling?"

"You don't think I'm repressed? Do you?"

"Very much so," said her companion, with mock solemnity. "But we can change all that. In the meantime, I feel a little offended that you shouldn't want to present me to your father."

"It isn't that. But I do feel"—she hesitated—"that he ought to have some *warning*. As a matter of fact"—again she hesitated—"I've sort of intimated to a friend of mine that he ought to—sort of break the news, you see? Before we get there."

Mr. Morell's eyebrows drew together.

"Oh? Which friend?"

"Fred Barlow."

Tony Morell reached into his waistcoat pocket, and fished out a pocket-piece, or mascot, which he had a habit of tossing up and catching when he was preoccupied or thinking. It was a bullet, a small revolver bullet. He said it had an interesting history, though Constance was not sure how a bullet could have an interesting history before it had been fired. He tossed it into the air, and caught it with a flat smack against his palm. He tossed it up and caught it again.

"Barlow," he repeated, turning his eyes sideways. "Isn't that the fellow who was in court? The fellow who defended that man your father just sentenced to death? The fellow your father wants you to marry?"

To her surprise, Constance saw that his face was suddenly white with what she knew must be jealousy. She thrilled to it with unholy pleasure; but she hastened to correct him.

"Tony dear, for the hundredth time I tell you there's nothing in it! I've never cared two pins for Freddie Barlow, and he knows it. I practically grew up with him! As for what Daddy wants—"

"Yes?"

"He wants what I want. Or at least I hope so." The brown eyes were uncertain. "Listen, dear. I wrote Fred a note. Usually, when a trial's over, the barristers all go into a place like a club locker-room, and take off those funny collars, and wash their hands, and argue. But I asked Fred to come straight out here as soon as he could get away. I said I had something terribly important to tell him." Her voice grew urgent and pleading. "Tony, he's coming now! You will be nice to him, won't you?"

Once more Tony Morell tossed the bullet into the air, caught it, and replaced it in his pocket. He glanced along the gravel path, where a figure in wig and gown was bearing down on them.

In person Frederick Barlow was long and lean, with a permanently satiric expression which indicated that he watched the world and discovered that it lacked much. In later years—if, for instance, he did not find the right sort of wife—this quality would turn to dry sourness on the bench. For he would probably be raised to the bench, one day.

His career was a triumph of bitter training over nature. By nature he was easy-going: but this, in law, must be crushed out and no nonsense about it. By nature he was a romantic: this must be crushed out even more quickly, unless it can be serviceable in addresses to the jury. He was known as a good business man, though he hated business more than anything else on earth. To become a KC at thirty-three is something of a minor miracle, and perhaps justifies self-discipline carried to the point of a mental hair shirt.

He came sauntering along the path, his black gown open and his thumbs hooked in his waistcoat pockets. His wig rode high on his head, with an open space above the ears which Constance had always thought rather absurd. His eyes, cat-green, were disconcerting to witnesses. He was smiling.

"Hello, old girl," he said, "I thought you were at Jane Tennant's house-party."

"We were," Constance answered rather breathlessly, "but Taunton's only a few miles from here, so we thought we'd come over and—and see how things were. Fred, this is Tony Morell."

Mr. Morell responded handsomely. He got up, wearing his most winning smile, and shook hands with effusive heartiness. But Constance was disturbed.

"I say, Fred. I'm sorry you lost your case."

"That's all right. Fortunes of war."

"I mean, I felt horribly sorry for that poor Lypiatt man. It made me half sick to watch him. Will he really—?"

"Hang?" supplied Barlow. "No. At least I don't think so."

"But the law—you heard what Daddy said—!"

Frederick Barlow whistled between his teeth, his expression only half interested. For he was watching Tony Morell.

"My dear Connie," he said, "that's your father's idea of playing cat-and-mouse. He doesn't care twopence about the law. What he is interested in is administering absolute, impartial justice as he sees it."

"But I still don't understand."

"Well, Lypiatt committed murder. If I read it rightly, your father doesn't think, under the circumstances, that Lypiatt ought to hang. On the other hand, he did commit murder and he deserves to be punished. So your respected parent will let him stew in his own juice as long as possible, thinking he's for the eight o'clock walk and the rope. Then Mr. Justice Ireton will formally approve the recommendation to mercy; and the Home Secretary will change the sentence to imprisonment for life. That's all."

Tony Morell's expressive face darkened. "Bit like the Inquisition, isn't it?"

"Perhaps. I don't know. Ask the judge."

"But has he the right to do a thing like that?" demanded Mr. Morell.

"Technically, yes."

"But morally?"

"Oh, morally!" said Barlow, with a dry smile and wave of his hand.

Constance felt that this interview was not going according to plan; that there were undercurrents she did not quite understand. She had an uneasy feeling that Fred Barlow half suspected what she was going to say. So she took the plunge.

"I'm glad to hear that. I mean, it would be a kind of bad omen, or leave a kind of bad taste, if something like that happened today. I'm terribly happy, Fred. Tony and I are engaged to be married."

This time Barlow thrust his hands into his trousers pockets. In spite of himself the blood rushed under his eyes; he seemed to hate this involuntary outward sign more than anything else. He hunched his shoulders under the black gown, looked at the ground, and teetered on his heels as though reflecting.

"Congratulations," he said. "Does the old man know?"

"No. We came up today to tell him, but you know how it is on the last day of assizes. He'll be going down to the seaside tonight, and we can see him there. But, Fred. You're going down to *your* cottage tonight, aren't you?"

"So you want me to break the news to him. Is that it?"

"Well, just sort of *hint* at it. Please, Fred! You will, won't you?"

"No," said Barlow after more reflection.

"You won't? But why not?"

Barlow grinned at her. Taking hold of the lapels of his gown as though he were addressing a jury, he put his head on one side and spoke mildly.

"For about twenty years," he said, "ever since you were learning to walk and I was a boy of twelve, I've fetched and carried for you. I did your sums and your French exercises when you were too lazy to do 'em yourself. Whenever you got into trouble, I squared it. You're a good-hearted wench, Connie, and your sex-appeal is limitless; but you never did have a sense of responsibility. If you're going to get married, you'll have to develop one. No. This is one piece of dirty work you must handle for yourself. And now you'll have to excuse me. I must get back to my client."

The girl sprang to her feet.

"You just don't care, do you?" she cried.

"Care?"

"You and Jane Tennant—" She checked herself. Then her voice poured with scorn. "And you're afraid of him too, like everybody else!"

Barlow did not answer. He directed towards Tony Morell something which was between a nod and a formal bow. Turning round, he walked back up the path at an unhurried pace. His gown billowed about him. Even the tail of his wig seemed eloquent.

Mr. Morell, who seemed to be darkly fuming over another matter, broke off and smiled at Constance.

"Never mind, my darling," he consoled her. "It's hardly his affair, is it? I can handle the matter, you know." The white teeth flashed.

"But, Tony. After all, you have got a dreadfully bad record, haven't you? In other people's eyes, I mean?"

"Alas!" said Mr. Morell humorously. His eyes narrowed. "Does it matter to you?"

The passion in her voice surprised even Mr. Morell.

"Not the least little bit in the world! I—I rather admire you for it. And, oh, Tony, I do love you so much! But"—again she hesitated, clicking open and shut the catch of her handbag—"but what *will* my father say?"

CHAPTER II

ON THE AFTERNOON OF THE FOLLOWING DAY, MR.
Justice Ireton sat in the living-room of his seaside bungalow,
playing chess with Dr. Gideon Fell.

It was not a very handsome bungalow, nor did it face
a very handsome stretch of beach. To find Horace Ireton
installed here might have surprised those friends who knew
his extreme fastidiousness and his catlike love of comfort. Mr. Justice Ireton loathed walking: when in London,
or on circuit, he never stirred a step where his limousine
could take him. He lived well up to—some said above—
his income. His town house in South Audley Street, his
country place in Berkshire, were fitted with the most syba-
ritic bathrooms and the most complicated of labour-saving
devices. He did himself well in the matter of eating and
drinking. His big cigars, his (genuine) Napoleon brandy,
and his fondness for French dishes were so well known
that no caricature of him ever failed to include at least
one of them.

But the truth is that Mr. Justice Ireton, like others of us, had illusions about sea air and the simple life.

Every year, usually about the end of the spring or the end of the summer, he began to have vague qualms about his health. These doubts were ill-founded. He had the digestion of an ostrich. But it was his habit to rent a cottage on some more or less remote strip of beach, far from seaside resorts, and remain there for several weeks or a month.

He did not go in for bathing: nobody had yet seen the probably awe-inspiring spectacle of Mr. Justice Ireton in a bathing-suit. As a rule he merely sat in a deckchair and owlishly read his favourite eighteenth-century authors. Sometimes, as an utmost concession to health, he would take a stroll along the sands at his stumpy, grudging walk, a cigar in his mouth and an expression of distaste on his face.

The Dunes, his present bungalow, was better than most of them. He had gone so far as to buy it because it had a tolerable bathroom. It was built of brick and yellow stucco, with French windows facing the sea. It contained two rooms, with a hall between, and kitchen and bathroom built out at the rear. In front of it, beyond a broad stretch of lawn where no human power could compel grass to grow, the asphalt road along the sea front ran east to the town of Tawnish and west to the curve of Horseshoe Bay. And on the other side of this road, past a scrubby tangle of what resembled grass grafted on seaweed, the bone-white beach sloped down to the sea.

The Dunes was the only house within half a mile of anybody or anything. No buses ran along the front of it, though it was in the Corporation area and they had condescended to light the road with a lamp every two hundred yards. In fine weather, with the sun on slate-blue water and the ochre-coloured promontory of Horseshoe Bay in the distance, the view was pleasant enough. But in murky weather it had a desolate, windblown look.

The afternoon was warm but faintly damp when Mr. Justice Ireton and Dr. Fell sat over the chess board in the living-room at The Dunes.

"Your move," said Mr. Justice Ireton patiently.

"Eh? Oh, ah!" said Dr. Fell, enlightened. He moved a piece rather wildly, for he was engrossed with some violence in the argument. "What I wish to know, sir, is this. Why? Why do you take such pleasure in these cat-and-mouse tactics? You intimate to me, softly, that young Lypiatt won't hang after all—"

"Check," said Mr. Justice Ireton, moving a piece.

"Eh?"

"Check!"

Distending his cheeks with a vast puff, Dr. Fell squared himself and scrutinized the board through eyeglasses on a broad black ribbon. He wheezed, through all twenty stone of him, and eyed his opponent suspiciously. His move was as defiant as the upthrust of his underlip.

"Harrumph, ha!" he growled. "But to return to the question. When the prisoner at the bar isn't in danger, you let him think he is. When he is in danger, you let him think he isn't. Do you remember the case of Dobbes, the Leadenhall Street swindler?"

"Check," said Mr. Justice Ireton, scooping his opponent's queen off the board.

"Oh? Have at you, then!—What about that?"

"Check."

"Archons of Athens! There doesn't seem to be...?"

"No," said the other. "Checkmate."

Gravely he gathered up the pieces and set them back in their places for the beginning of play. But he did not suggest another game.

"You're a bad chess player," he said. "You won't concentrate. Now, then. What was it you wanted to know?"

If in court he had seemed remote, sitting up there as detached as a Yogi, here he appeared more human though even less approachable. Yet he was a good, easy host. He wore a tweed sports coat and plus-fours—which looked incongruous—and sat forward in the overstuffed chair so that his short legs could reach the ground.

"May I speak frankly, then?" demanded Dr. Fell.

"Yes."

"You see," explained Dr. Fell, getting out a bandana handkerchief and mopping his forehead with such earnestness that even the judge smiled, "it takes a bit of doing to come out flat with it. You're rather a gimlet-eye, you know. Or at least you have that reputation."

"So I understand."

"And do you remember Dobbes, the City swindler?"

"Perfectly."

"Well," admitted Dr. Fell, "you made *me* shiver, at least. Dobbes, with his small investors' racket, was a nasty bit of work. I cheerfully admit that. When he came up before you for sentence, he deserved a stiff dose and knew he was going to get it. You talked to him, in that quiet way of yours, until he nearly fainted. Then you gave him his sentence—five years—and motioned the warders to take him away. We could almost see the wretch stagger with relief at getting so little as five years.

"We thought it was all over. So did the warders. So did Dobbes. You let him get as far as the stairs down from the dock before you said: 'Just one moment, Mr. Dobbes. There is another count against you. You had better come back.' Back he came, and got five years more. And then," said Dr. Fell, "when Dobbes broke down, and those of us who were watching wanted to drop through the floor out of sight, you did it for the third time. Total: fifteen years."

Mr. Justice Ireton picked up a chess piece off the board, turned it over in his small plump fingers, and replaced it.

"Well?" he said.

"No comment occurs to you?"

"The maximum penalty for Dobbes's offences," observed Mr. Justice Ireton, "would have been twenty years."

"Sir," said Dr. Fell, with polished courtesy, "you don't maintain that the sentence was a merciful one?"

The judge smiled slightly. "No," he said; "I didn't mean it to be. But twenty years would have been too much for what I believed to be strict justice. Therefore he didn't get it."

"And the cat-and-mouse business..."

"Can you deny he deserved it?"

"No; but—"

"Then, my dear doctor, what are you complaining about?"

The living-room at The Dunes was a spacious oblong room, with three French windows opening on the side towards the sea. Its wallpaper was bilious; and, since Mr. Justice Ireton had taken over the furniture from the late owner until he could put in some of his own, this must have provided him with moments of aesthetic agony.

On the wall opposite the windows hung a stuffed moose's head, with staring glass eyes. Under this was a Victorian desk complete with swivel-chair, though it boasted a telephone. On the sofa and one of the easychairs were cushions sewn with such bead designs as *Home Sweet Home*, and a curved pipe topped by unconvincing-looking smoke. The only signs of Mr. Justice Ireton's tenancy were the piles of books stacked into corners.

Dr. Fell never forgot the round, sleek little judge sitting among these gimcracks, and speaking in that soft snappish voice of his.

"I don't like the subject," he continued. "And, frankly, sir, I resent being questioned about it—"

Dr. Fell grunted guiltily.

"But, since you've begun it, you may as well know my views. The state pays me to do my job. I do it as I see fit. That's all."

"The job being?"

"To judge, of course!" said the other simply. "To see that juries don't go wrong."

"But suppose *you* make a mistake?"

Mr. Justice Ireton stretched out his arms, flexing the muscles.

"I am young, as jurists go," he said. "Only sixty last month. But I think I am pretty tough. I also think I am pretty difficult to deceive. That may be vanity. Still, there it is."

Dr. Fell seemed to be afflicted with strange internal rumblings.

"If you will pardon my own candour," he replied, "what interests me is this rigid Roman spirit of yours. It is admirable. No doubt! But (just between ourselves) don't you ever have any qualms? Can't you ever see yourself in the position of the man in the dock? Don't you ever have the Christian humility to shiver and say to yourself, 'There, but for the grace of God—'?"

The other's sleepy eyes opened.

"No. Why should I? That is no concern of mine."

"Sir," said Dr. Fell gravely, "you are a superman. Mr. Shaw has been looking for you for years."

"Not at all," said the judge. "I am a realist."

Again he smiled slightly.

"Doctor," he went on, "hear me out. I have been accused of many things in my time, but never of being a hypocrite or a stuffed shirt. So, I say: hear me out. Now, why should I murmur any such pious catchword as you suggest? *I* am not likely to rob my neighbour's till, or murder my neighbour in order to get his wife. My income precludes the first temptation, and my common sense the second."

He made one of those gestures which were all the more compelling for being so restrained.

"But observe. I worked—hard!—to achieve both my income and my common sense. Unfortunately, the criminals of this world won't do that. They have no more right to behave as they like than I have. They have no more right to lose their heads than I have. But they do. And then they beg for mercy. They will not get it from me."

The level voice stopped. Mr. Justice Ireton picked up a chess piece from the board, and set it down again flatly; as though he had signed and sealed a document, and now wished to be done with it.

"Well," mused Dr. Fell, smoothing his moustache, "that would seem to be that. So you couldn't, for instance, imagine yourself committing a crime?"

The judge reflected.

"Under certain circumstances, I might. Though I doubt it. But if I did—"

"Yes?"

"I should weigh up the chances. If they were strongly in my favour, I might take the risk. If they were not in my favour, I should not take it. But one thing I should not do. I should not go off half-cocked, and then whine that I wasn't guilty and that 'circumstantial evidence' was against me. Unfortunately, that's what they all do—the lot of them."

"Forgive my curiosity," said Dr. Fell politely. "But did you ever try an innocent man?"

"Frequently. And I flatter myself that he was always acquitted."

Suddenly Mr. Justice Ireton chuckled.

Not for days had he been so talkative. Outside the court-room he rarely uttered three sentences on end. Gideon Fell was an acquaintance of many years' standing; but at first, at the end of a long and wearisome assizes, Horace Ireton had been inclined to resent this visit of the doctor, who was staying at Tawnish and had dropped in to pay his respects. Now, however, he did not resent it at all. He had talked himself into a good humour.

"Come!" he said. "I'm not an ogre, my dear Fell. You know that."

"Oh, ah. I know that."

"And I even hope, outside business hours, that I'm a reasonably good fellow. Which reminds me." He looked at his watch. "I won't offer you tea, because Mrs. Drew is out and I hate fiddling about in the kitchen; but what do you say to a whisky and soda?"

"Thank'ee. That," said Dr. Fell, "is an invitation I seldom refuse."

"Your views on criminology," pursued the judge, getting up briskly and stumping across to the sideboard; "your views on criminology, in general, are sound. I admit that. But you can't play chess. Now that gambit I caught you with—eh?"

"I suppose it was your own particular brand and development of dirty work?"

"If you like. It consists in letting your opponent think he's perfectly safe, winning hands down: and then catching him in a corner. You would probably call it the cat-and-mouse gambit."

Mr. Justice Ireton held up two glasses to the light, inspecting them to see that they were clean. As he put them down again his glance wandered round the room. He eyed with distaste the radiant overstuffed furniture, the cushions, and the stuffed moose's head; his small nose wrinkled. But he evidently decided that it was all in a good cause, for he sniffed deeply of the sea air that blew in through one of the partly open French windows, and he grew resigned. What pronouncement he was about to add, as he poured out two rather large whiskies, Dr. Fell never learned.

"*Hello, there!*" cried a voice. "*Coo-ee!*"

It was a girl's voice, calling with a sort of desperate sprightliness. Dr. Fell was startled.

"Guests?" he inquired. "Female guests?"

A shade of exasperation crossed Mr. Justice Ireton's face.

"I imagine it's my daughter. Though what she's doing here I don't know. I heard of her last at a house-party in Taunton. Yes?"

A fair-haired girl, wearing one of the transparent picture-hats which were fashionable in that year nineteen thirty-six, stepped in through the open window. She also wore a thin flowered frock, and twisted a white handbag in rather uncertain fingers. Dr. Fell observed with pleasure that she had honest brown eyes, though it seemed to even his uncritical gaze that she was somewhat heavily made up.

"Hello!" she added with the same desperate sprightliness. "Here I am!"

Mr. Justice Ireton's manner became dry and formal.

"So I observe," he said. "And to what do I owe this unexpected honour?"

"I had to come down," the girl said defensively. Then, as though breaking loose, she went on with a rush. "I've got the most wonderful news. I'm engaged to be married."

CHAPTER III

Constance had not meant to blurt it out like this.

But even at the last minute she had not been able to make up her mind how to approach him.

Constance, a guilty reader of romantic fiction, had tried to decide how he would act according to what she had read or seen at the films. In the stories, fathers were divided into only two classes. Either they were furious or implacable, or else they were almost unbelievably wise and sympathetic. Either they tossed you out of the house straight away, or they patted your hand and spoke words of whimsical wisdom. And Constance (like perhaps every other girl who has ever lived) felt that her own parent simply would not fit into either of these two categories. Were *all* parents so difficult? Or only just her own?

Her father was standing by the sideboard, his hand on the soda-syphon.

"Engaged?" he repeated. Then she was astonished to see colour come into his pale face; and to hear his voice, from surprise, grow warm with pleasure.

"Engaged to be married? To Fred Barlow? My dear Constance! I congrat—"

Constance's heart sank.

"No, Daddy. Not to Fred. It's—it's somebody you haven't met."

"Oh," said Mr. Justice Ireton.

Dr. Fell, who is not without tact of a clumsy sort, saved the situation then. Though his presence in any drawing-room is about as inconspicuous as that of a well-grown elephant, the girl had not noticed him. He called attention to his presence by a long, rumbling throat-clearing. Surging to his feet with the aid of his crutch-handled stick, he beamed and twinkled down at both of them.

"If you don't mind," he said, "I won't have that drink after all. I promised Inspector Graham that I would drop in about tea time, and it's past that already. Harrumph."

Mr. Justice Ireton spoke mechanically.

"My daughter. Dr. Gideon Fell."

Constance flashed him a brief smile, startled but still hardly seeing him.

"If you really feel you must go?" suggested the judge, obviously relieved.

"Afraid so. We'll continue the debate another time. Hey?"

Dr. Fell picked up his box-pleated cape from the sofa, swung it round his shoulders, and fastened it with the little chain. Wheezing with the labour of so much effort, he put on and adjusted his shovel-hat. Then, raising his stick in salute, and with a bow to Constance, which added several new ridges to his waistcoat, he blundered out through the French window. Father and daughter watched him go down the lawn, and make a sort of safe-breaking operation out of getting the gate open.

During a long silence, Mr. Justice Ireton went across to his chair and sat down.

Constance felt as though someone were squeezing her heart.

"Daddy—" she began.

"One moment," said her father. "Before you tell me about it, be good enough to take some of that makeup off your face. You look like a street-walker."

This was the sort of approach which always drove Constance mad.

"Won't you ever," she cried, "won't you *ever* take me seriously?"

"If," answered the judge dispassionately, "anyone took you seriously in your present appearance, he would expect you to call him 'dearie' and ask for a quid. Remove the mask, please."

He could be as patient as a spider. The silence lengthened. In desperation Constance took a compact out of her handbag, opened it to peer at the mirror, and swabbed first at her lips and then at her cheeks with a handkerchief. When she had concluded, she felt dishevelled both in mind and body.

Mr. Justice Ireton nodded.

"Now," he said. "I presume you mean what you say? You're quite serious about this?"

"Daddy, I was never so terribly serious in my life!"

"Well?"

"Well, what?"

"Who is he?" asked the judge patiently. "What do you know about him? What's his background?"

"His—his name is Anthony Morell. I met him in London."

"Yes. What does he do for a living?"

"He's part owner of a nightclub. At least, that's one of the things he does."

Mr. Justice Ireton closed his eyes briefly, and opened them again.

"What else does he do?"

"I don't know. But he's got lots and lots of money."

"Who are his parents?"

"I don't know. They're dead."

"Where did you meet him?"

"At a party in Chelsea."

"How long have you known him?"

"Two months, at least."

"Have you slept with him?"

"Daddy!"

Constance was genuinely shocked. She was shocked not at the suggestion, which she would have accepted with equanimity or even complacency from anyone else, but at the fact that it came from him.

Mr. Justice Ireton's mild eyes opened. "I asked you a simple question," he pointed out. "Surely you can answer it. Have you?"

"No."

Though not a muscle in the judge's face moved, he seemed to be expelling his breath. He relaxed a little, putting his hands flat along the arms of the chair.

Constance, though befuddled, noticed that at least the most ominous danger-sign of all his moods was not present. He did not take his shell-rimmed spectacles out of their case in his breast pocket, put them on and take them off deliberately, as his habit was when on the bench. But she felt that she could not stand this impassivity.

"Can't you say anything?" she pleaded. "Please say you don't mind! If you tried to stop me from marrying Tony, I think I'd just die!"

"You are twenty-one years old," the judge pointed out. He reflected. "In fact, you came into your mother's money only six months ago."

"Five hundred a year!" said the girl contemptuously.

"I was not commenting on the inadequacy, to you, of the amount. I was stating the fact. You are twenty-one and independent. If you chose to marry, I couldn't prevent you."

"No; but you could—"

"What?"

"I don't know!" said Constance miserably. After a pause she added: "Can't you *say* something?"

"If you like." He was silent for a time. Then he put his fingers to his temples, and ruffled the fingers across his forehead. "I must confess I had hoped you would marry young Barlow. He has a tremendous future ahead of him, I think, if he keeps his head. I've advised him, even trained him, for years—"

(Yes, thought Constance, and that's just the trouble! Mr. Barlow—when she wanted to be particularly severe, she always thought of him as "Mr."—was growing more like his tutor every day; was growing old before his time. Let the bouncing Jane Tennant, who obviously adored him, have Fred Barlow. Facing life with a man who had been trained by her fish-blooded father was more than Constance thought she could put up with.)

Mr. Justice Ireton pondered.

"Your mother," he said, "was in many ways a very silly woman—"

"Don't you *dare* talk like that about her!"

"Indeed. You were too young to remember your mother, I think?"

"Yes; but—"

"Then be good enough not to voice an opinion when you have no adequate basis for judgment. Your mother, I say, was in many ways a very silly woman. In many ways she irritated me. When she died I was sorry, though I can't say I was grief-stricken. But you—!"

He shifted in his chair. Constance spoke breathlessly.

"Well? Are you going to play cat-and-mouse with me too? Won't you say something one way or the other? Won't you at least meet Tony?"

The judge looked up quickly.

"Oh? Is he here?"

"He's down on the beach, throwing stones at the water. I thought I'd see you first, and sort of prepare you; and then he could come up and talk to you."

"Very commendable. Will you ask him to come up, then?"

"But if you—"

"My dear Constance, what do you expect me to say? 'Yes' or 'no,' 'God bless you,' or 'It won't do,' without any information? Your biographical sketch of Mr. Morell, you will admit, was not very comprehensive. By all means have him up! I shall be able to form an opinion about this gentleman after I have met him."

Constance turned away, and then hesitated. It seemed to her that there had been a soft, sinister emphasis on the word "gentleman." As usual after a meeting with her father, she had a hot, resentful feeling that all her meanings had been twisted and all her straight questions evaded: that she had got nowhere.

"Daddy," she said abruptly, with her hand on the window, "there's one other thing."

"Yes?"

"I'm bound to tell you, because I want to ask you (please, for heaven's sake) to be fair! I don't think you're going to like Tony, really."

"No?"

"But if you don't like him, it'll be because of a lot of prejudices and nothing else. For instance, Tony likes bottle-parties, and dancing, and modern things. He's terribly intelligent—"

"Indeed?" said Mr. Justice Ireton.

"But he likes modern authors and composers. He says the things you and Fred Barlow have tried to get me to admire are so much dreary rubbish. And one thing more. He's had— well, escapades; yes, and I admire him for it? Can he help it if women find him so attractive? Can he help it if they throw themselves at his head?"

"I don't know," said her father imperturbably. "You will give me a better opportunity to find out if you ask him to come up here."

Again Constance hesitated.

"Would you like me to be here when you talk to him?"

"No."

"Oh. Well, I'd rather not be here, either."

She scuffed with her slipper at the bottom of the French window, peering hesitantly back at him. "I'll just sort of hang about, then." She clenched her fists. "But you *will* be nice to him, won't you?"

"I will deal fairly with him, Constance. I promise you that."

The girl turned and ran.

Shadows were gathering in the room, and across road and beach and sea. The sun, fiery red and half blotted out, emerged from behind clouds low down along the water. It kindled the room and then was hidden again, smudgily. The turn of the dusk brought a damp smell, mingled with the iodine-tang of seaweed, sweeping up on a breeze from the south. In that momentary glow of sun, the far edges of the beach showed flat and grey and glistening where the tide was out; but the breeze already carried, against a vast hush, the soft, snaky hiss of the tide coming in.

Mr. Justice Ireton stirred in his chair.

He got up rather stiffly, and went to the sideboard. He contemplated the two untasted whiskies he had poured out. After considering them, he picked up one glass, emptied its contents into the other, and added soda. From a box on the sideboard he took a cigar, tore off its band, clipped it, and lighted it. When it was drawing to his satisfaction, he returned to his chair carrying the whisky glass. He set the glass down on the edge of the chess table, and continued to smoke placidly.

Brisk footsteps sounded in the patchy lawn outside.

"Good evening, sir!" said the subdued but hearty voice of Mr. Anthony Morell. "Come to beard the lion in his den, you see!"

Thick-set and ingratiating, sweeping off his hat as he entered, Mr. Morell advanced, smiling, with extended hand.

CHAPTER IV

"Good evening," said the judge. He shook the extended hand, not enthusiastically, without getting up. "Will you sit down?"

"Thanks."

"Across from me, please. Where I can get a look at you."

"Oh. Right-o."

Tony Morell sat down. The overstuffed chair tilted him backwards, and he instantly sat upright again, as though not to be put at a disadvantage.

Mr. Justice Ireton continued to smoke with placid deliberation. He did not say anything. His small eyes were fixed steadily on his guest's face. It was a regard which might have paralysed a sensitive man: as perhaps Morell was.

Morell cleared his throat.

"I suppose," he observed, speaking suddenly into a great silence, "Connie's told you?"

"Told me what?"

"About us."

"What, in particular, about you? Try to be precise."

"The marriage!"

"Oh. Yes. She's told me. Will you have a cigar? Or a whisky and soda?"

"No, thank you, sir," replied Morell, firing back the answer instantly and with somewhat self-conscious complacency. "I never use tobacco or spirits. This is my tipple."

As though encouraged or emboldened by the invitation, he seemed more at ease. He had the air of a man whose hand conceals the ace of trumps, and who is wondering only about the proper time to play it. But he made no move of this kind. Instead he produced a packet of chewing-gum, which he displayed to his host before removing the tissue-paper from a stick of it, and crumpling it into his mouth with manifest pleasure.

Mr. Justice Ireton did not say anything.

"Not that I've got any objections to 'em," Mr. Morell assured him, alluding to the tobacco and the spirits. "Just don't use 'em."

After this magnanimous explanation, he fell silent for what seemed to him an uncomfortable moment. Then he plunged in.

"Now about Connie and me. She's been a bit worried about it; but I told her I thought I could persuade you to be reasonable. We don't want trouble. We want you to be our friend, if you will. You haven't any real objection to our getting married; now have you?"

He smiled.

The judge took the cigar out of his mouth.

"You see no objection yourself?" he asked.

Morell hesitated.

"Well," he admitted, frowning his swarthy forehead into horizontal wrinkles, "there is one thing. You see, I'm a Roman Catholic. I'm afraid I must insist that we be married in the Catholic Church, and that Connie becomes a Catholic herself. You understand, don't you?"

The judge inclined his head.

"Yes. You are good enough to say that you will marry my daughter provided she changes her religion."

"Oh, look here, sir! I don't want you to suggest—"

"I am not suggesting anything. I am merely repeating what you said."

Very deliberately he reached into the breast pocket of his coat. He took his shell-rimmed spectacles from their case, fitted them on, and looked at Morell through them. Then he took them off and began to swing them, gently, in his left hand.

"But there are ways of putting these things!" complained Morell. He fidgeted. Real hostility began to grow in his prominent, dark, sensitive eyes. "After all, religion is a serious matter to me. It is to all Catholics. I only—"

"Let us leave that, if you please. You see no objection to this marriage, say, from my point of view?"

"No; not really."

"You're quite sure of that?"

"Well, maybe there's one thing I ought to tell you—"

"You don't need to tell me. I know."

"You know what?"

Mr. Justice Ireton put down his cigar on the edge of the chess table. He shifted his glasses to his right hand and continued to swing them gently, though a close observer would have seen that the hand trembled a little.

"Antonio Morelli," he said. "Sicilian by birth. Naturalized British—I forget when. Five years ago, at Kingston assizes, this Antonio Morelli appeared before my friend Mr. Justice Wythe."

There was a silence.

"I don't know," Morell said slowly, "where you got hold of that old piece of muck. But, if you know anything about the case, you'll know that *I'm* the one who ought to complain. I was the injured party. I was the victim."

"Yes. No doubt. Let me see if I can recall the facts." Mr. Justice Ireton pursed his lips. "The case interested me, because it bore a curious parallel to the case of Madeleine Smith and Pierre L'Angelier: though you, Mr. Morell, fared rather better than L'Angelier.

"This Antonio Morelli became engaged, in secret, to the daughter of a wealthy and influential family. There was talk of marriage. She wrote him a number of letters of the sort that some jurists feel bound to describe as scandalous. Then the girl's ardour began to cool. Whereupon Morelli intimated that, unless she kept her promise and made an honest man of him, he would show the letters to her father. The girl lost her head and tried to shoot Morelli. The charge was one of attempted murder, of which she was acquitted."

"That's a lie," said Morell, half getting up and breathing the words into the judge's face.

"A lie?" repeated Mr. Justice Ireton, putting on his spectacles. "A lie that the girl was acquitted?"

"You know what I mean!"

"I'm afraid I don't."

"I didn't want the woman. She ran after me. I couldn't help it. Then, when the little idiot tried to kill me because I wasn't having any, her family had to cook up some story to get sympathy for her. That's all there was to it. I never made any such threat, or thought of making any." He paused, and added significantly: "Connie knows all about it, by the way."

"No doubt. Do you deny the truth of the evidence that was presented at the trial?"

"Yes, I do. It was circumstantial evidence. It...what's the matter with you? Why are you looking like that?"

"Nothing. Pray go on. I have heard the story before; but go on."

Morell sat back, breathing slowly and heavily. He passed a hand across his hair. The chewing-gum, which he had lodged for safety in one corner of his mouth, now came into play again. His square, close-shaven jaws champed with steady rhythm, and he made a clicking noise with the gum.

"You think you've got me sized up, don't you?" he demanded.

"Yes."

"And if you were wrong?"

"I will risk that. Mr. Morell, this interview has already gone on long enough; and it has been, I need hardly tell you, the most distasteful of my life. I had only one more question to ask you. How much?"

"Eh?"

"How much money," explained the judge, with patient elucidation, "will you require to go away and let my daughter alone for good?"

Shadows were deepening in the room, and the air had turned chilly. A curious smile travelled across Morell's face, showing the strong white teeth. He drew a deep breath. It was as though he were shaking off a difficult role, like a man getting rid of an uncomfortable garment. He settled back in the chair, shaking his shoulders.

"After all," he smiled, "business is business. Isn't it?"

Mr. Justice Ireton closed his eyes.

"Yes."

"But I'm very fond of Connie. So it would have to be a good offer: a *very* good offer." He made the gum click. "What are you prepared to pay?"

"No," said the judge dispassionately. "State your terms. You mustn't ask me to assess your worth. After all, I don't really expect you to accept two shillings or half a crown."

"Ah, but that's where you're wrong!" the other pointed out agreeably. "It's not, fortunately, a question of my worth. It's a question of Connie's worth. She's a fine girl, you know; and it would be a shame if you, her father, were to cheapen her by underestimating her value. Yes. You must be prepared to pay a reasonable price for her, plus a little legitimate profit for my injured heart. Shall we say"—he considered, walking his fingers along the arm of the chair, and then looking up—"five thousand pounds?"

"Don't be a fool."

"Isn't she worth that much to you?"

"It is not a question of what she's worth to me. It's a question of how much I can raise."

"Is that so?" inquired Morell with interest, eyeing him sideways. The smile flickered again. "Well, I've had my say.

If you want to continue this discussion, I'm afraid you must come to me with an offer."

"A thousand pounds."

Morell laughed at him. "Don't *you* be a fool, my dear sir. Connie's got five hundred a year of her own."

"Two thousand."

"No. Not good enough. Now if you were to say three thousand, cash, I might consider it. I don't say I would; but I *might*."

There was a silence.

"Well," said Morell, shrugging his shoulders, "all right. It's too bad you don't value her any higher than that, as you'll find to your cost; but I know when I've got a customer to the breaking-point."

(Mr. Justice Ireton made a slight, short movement.)

"Agreed at three thousand," concluded Morell, chewing with decision. "When can I have the money?"

"There will be conditions."

"Conditions?"

"I mean to make very certain you don't trouble my daughter again."

For a good business man, Morell seemed strangely incurious about these conditions.

"Suit yourself," he conceded. "I want to see the money on the table, that's all. In cash. So—when?"

"I don't keep a sum like that in my current account. I shall want twenty-four hours to raise the money. One little point, Mr. Morell. Constance is down on the beach now. What if I were to call her up here and tell her about this transaction?"

"She wouldn't believe you," answered Morell promptly, "and you know it. As a matter of fact, she's been expecting you to try some sort of trick. A statement like that would finish you in her eyes. Don't try it on, my dear sir, or I'll upset your applecart and marry her tomorrow. You can tell her about my—er—perfidy after I've seen the colour of your money. Not until then."

"That," said the judge in a curious voice, "will suit me."

"Well? Delivery?"

The judge reflected. "You are at this house-party in Taunton, I take it?"

"Yes."

"Could you come up here tomorrow night about eight o'clock?"

"With pleasure."

"Have you got a car?"

"Alas, no!"

"No matter. There is a bus between Taunton and Tawnish every hour. The seven o'clock will get you to the Market Square in Tawnish by eight. The last half-mile you'll have to do on foot. Simply walk out of Tawnish and follow the sea-front road until you get here."

"I know. Connie and I made the trip today."

"Don't come before then, because I may not be back from London. And—you'll have to think up some excuse to give Constance as to why you're leaving the house-party."

"I'm an adept at that. Never fear. Well…"

He got up, brushing his coat. The room was full of twilight, so it is to be feared that neither of them noticed the expression on the other's face. Both of them seemed to be listening to the faint, soft thunder of the tide coming in.

From his waistcoat pocket Morell fished out a tiny object

which he balanced in his palm. It was too dark for the judge to make out what it was: it was the small-calibre revolver-bullet Morell carried as a pocket-piece. He fingered it lovingly, as though it had brought him luck.

"It's your show," he observed, not without malice; "and I wish you joy of it. But—Connie's down there now. We're supposed to be arriving at a decision. What are you going to tell her?"

"I shall tell her that I approve of the marriage."

"Oh?" Morell stiffened. "Why?"

"What other course do you leave me? If I forbid it, she will ask for reasons. If I give those reasons…"

"Yes, there's that." Morell reflected. "And her face will light up—I can imagine it—and for twenty-four hours she'll be perfectly happy. Then amputation with a smile. Bit cruel, don't you think?"

"*You* talk of cruelty?"

"In any case," said the other, with an unabashed coolness, "it will do my heart good to hear you give us your blessing, and see you shake hands with me. I'm going to insist you shake hands with me. And promise to stump up a fish-slice for the nuptials. It seems too bad you've got to subject Connie to this; but please yourself. Well, shall I go and call her?"

"Do."

"Then here goes." Morell dropped the bullet back in his pocket and put on his rakish hat. He stood framed against the pale light from the windows, in a light grey suit too much pinched in at the waist. "And the next time you see me, mind you call me 'my dear boy.'"

"One moment," said the judge without moving. "Suppose by some unforeseen chance I couldn't raise the money?"

"That," Morell pointed out, "would be just too bad. Goodbye."

He gave a final click of the gum, and went out.

Mr. Justice Ireton sat still as though considering. He stretched out his hand, picked up the untasted double-whisky from the table, and drained it. His cigar, put down and forgotten, had gone out. With an effort he pushed himself to his feet, and went slowly across to the desk against the wall. Pushing aside the telephone, he opened the top drawer of the desk and drew out a folded letter.

It was too dark for him to read the letter, but he knew every line of it. It was from the manager of his branch of the City and Provincial Bank. Though framed in terms of the utmost respect, it made plain that the bank could not consent to carry any further Mr. Justice Ireton's already considerable overdraft. Touching the matter of the mortgages on the houses in South Audley Street and in Frey, Berkshire—

He spread the letter out on the desk. Then he changed his mind and threw it back into the drawer, which he closed.

Night-noises whispered up from the sea. Far away, there was the throb of a motor car. To anybody who saw him then (but nobody did see him) the change in Horace Ireton's behaviour would have been almost shocking. His stout body seemed to grow as limp as a laundry-bag. Removing his spectacles, he pressed his fingers over his eyes. Once he lifted both fists, as though for a wordless cry which he did not utter.

Then footsteps, the murmur of voices, and Constance's rather forced laughter, warned him that the two were returning.

He put on his spectacles again, with great deliberation, and turned round in the chair.

That was Friday evening, the twenty-seventh of April. On the following night, Mr. Anthony Morell reached Tawnish not by bus, but by the eight o'clock train from London. In the Market Square he inquired his way to the coast road. Another witness testified that he reached the judge's bungalow at twenty-five minutes past eight. At half past eight (clocked by the telephone exchange) somebody fired a shot. Mr. Morell died there of a bullet through the brain; and, until it was too late, the murderer never knew what was in his victim's pocket.

CHAPTER V

THE GIRL AT THE TELEPHONE EXCHANGE WAS READING *True Sex-Life Stories.*

Florence sometimes wondered whether these stories were really true. But of course the magazine wouldn't dare print them unless they were; and they sounded true, too. With a sigh of envy, Florence thought that the girls in the stories, no matter how irretrievably ruined, always managed to have such a good time. Nobody had ever offered to ruin *her* in so many interesting ways. And this white-slave business, though no doubt it was all very terrible, still...

The switchboard buzzed, and the red light came on.

Florence plugged in, with another sigh. She hoped it wasn't like that call a few minutes ago, when a woman had rung up from a public callbox and wanted to put through a toll call without any money. Florence didn't like women anyway. But the girls in these stories certainly did see life, even though of course they repented afterwards. They went to fashionable gambling-houses. They met gangsters, and got mixed up in murders...

"Number, please?" said Florence.

There was no reply.

In the little room, a loud-ticking clock said that it was eight-thirty. Florence found it soothing. Its ticking went on during a long silence, while Florence dreamed and the line remained open.

"Number, please," repeated Florence, waking up.

Then it happened.

A man's voice, speaking very low but with desperate hurry, whispered, "*The Dunes. Ireton's cottage. Help!*" And these gabbling words were followed by the revolver shot.

Florence did not at the moment identify it as a revolver shot. She only knew that, in the earphones, the carbon cracked against her ears with a physical pain which made her feel that steel needles were being driven into her brain. As she jumped up from the switchboard she heard a moan, a scuffle, and a rattling thud.

Then silence, while the clock ticked.

Though Florence felt sheer panic, she kept her head. For a short time she held to the desk and looked at the clock as though for inspiration. She nodded to herself. Her fingers flew to plug in another number.

"Tawnish police station," answered a young but rather self-important voice. "PC Weems speaking."

"Albert—"

The voice changed. "Didn't I tell you," it said in an urgent mutter, "never to ring up here when—"

"But, Albert, it's not that! It's horrible things."

Florence told him what she had heard. "I thought I'd better—"

"Very good, miss. Thank you. We'll attend to it."

At the other end of the line PC Weems hung up the receiver in consternation mingled with doubt. He repeated the story to his sergeant, who scratched a heavy chin and hesitated.

"The judge!" he said. "Probably nothing in it. But if somebody *has* tried to kill the old boy: crumbs, we're for it! Hop on your bike, Bert, and get out there as fast as you can. Hurry!"

PC Weems hopped. From Tawnish police station to the judge's cottage was about three-quarters of a mile. Weems would have made it in four minutes if he had not met with an interruption.

It was well after dark. There had been rain earlier in the evening; and, though it had now cleared up, the warm spring night was moonless and damp. Ahead of Weems's bicycle lamp the asphalt road gleamed black along the sea front. Street lamps at a distance of two hundred yards only intensified and distorted the darkness. They looked wind-blown, like sea-front trees; the tang of the sea was pungent, and Weems's ears were full of the shaky thunder of breakers at high tide.

He could discern the lights of the judge's cottage, some distance down on his right, when he became aware of the lights of a motor car blazing at him from close at hand. The car was parked on the wrong side of the road.

"Constable!" called a man's voice. "I say, constable!"

Weems instinctively pulled up, sliding one foot to the ground to steady himself.

"I was coming to tell you," the voice went on. "There's a tramp—drunk—Dr. Fellows and I…"

Now Weems recognized the voice. It belonged to Mr. Fred

Barlow, who himself owned a cottage farther along in the direction of Horseshoe Bay. For Mr. Barlow young Weems had a vast if puzzled respect, a respect eclipsed only by the awe he felt for the judge.

"Can't stop now, sir," he gasped, between excitement and loss of breath. His self-importance led him to impart a confidence to Mr. Barlow, as being worthy of it. "There's been trouble at Mr. Justice Ireton's place."

The voice came sharply out of the darkness.

"Trouble?"

"A shooting," said Weems, "the telephone operator thinks. Somebody's been shot."

As he raised himself on pedal and handlebars, Weems saw Mr. Barlow move round the car into the glow of the lamps. He was afterwards to remember the expression of Mr. Barlow's lean face, illuminated down one side; with the mouth half open and the eyelids pinched. Mr. Barlow wore a sports jacket, soiled flannels, and no hat.

"Go on!" Barlow said grimly. "Go like the devil! I'm right behind you."

Pedalling hard, Weems saw his companion was keeping up with him at a long, effortless stride. It seemed to Weems rather undignified that anybody should be running along beside the law like this. It shocked him. He pedalled harder to get away, but still the figure kept up. Weems was panting when he tumbled off the bicycle at Mr. Justice Ireton's gate—to meet with another encounter.

Constance Ireton, dim and white in the darkness, stood just inside the gate. Her figure twisted and untwisted round the wooden palings; the wind ruffled her hair and blew her frock against her body. By the light of the bicycle lamp Weems could see that she was crying.

Barlow merely stood and stared at her; it was the constable who spoke.

"Miss," he said, "what is it?"

"I don't know," answered Constance. "I don't *know*. You'd better go up there. No, don't go up there!"

She stretched out her hand, ineffectually, as Weems opened the gate. The living-room of the bungalow was a blaze of light; all three French windows were uncurtained, and one stood partly open. They could see the sparse grass and damp ground outside. With Barlow following him, Weems ran to the open window.

PC Albert Weems was conscientious, he was hard-working: he was even, at times, clumsily imaginative. On the way out he had been picturing what might have happened here. These images chiefly consisted of murderous attempts on the life of the judge, in which he might arrive in time to be the hero of the occasion by nabbing the criminal, overpowering him in a standup fight, and grasping the hand of a victim who should at least live long enough to express gratitude in the proper quarters.

But it was not what he saw.

A dead man—dead as mutton—lay face downwards on the floor in front of the desk across the room. It was not Mr. Justice Ireton. It was a black-haired man in a grey suit. He had been shot through the back of the head, just behind the right ear.

The light of the desk lamp, yellow and clear, showed the clean-punctured hole in the hair-line, with a little sluggish blood. The dead man's fingers were spread out on the carpet like talons, the skin wrinkling along the backs of the hands. The desk chair had been overturned. The telephone had been knocked off the desk; it lay beside the victim, its receiver still off the hook and clicking angrily beside the dead man's ear.

But this was not what froze PC Weems with horror, so that he could not believe his eyes. It was the sight of Mr. Justice Ireton sitting in an easychair, some half a dozen feet from the dead man, with a revolver in his hand.

Mr. Justice Ireton breathed slowly and heavily. His face was the colour of dough, though his little eyes were calm and seemed to be turned inwards. The revolver, a small one, was of polished steel with a black hard-rubber grip; it glittered under the desk lamp and the central chandelier. As though conscious for the first time he was holding the revolver, Mr. Justice Ireton stretched out his hand and dropped it with a small rattle on the chess table beside him.

PC Weems heard that noise, as he heard the drag and thunder of the surf beyond the windows. But both noises were meaningless. Both occurred in a void. His first words—blurted and instinctive—were remembered by the others long afterwards.

"*Sir, what have you gone and done?*"

The judge drew a deep breath. He fixed his little eyes on Weems, and cleared his throat.

"A most improper question," he said.

Relief flooded Weems.

"I know!" Weems said, noting the colour and contour of the face that was pressed against the carpet, and the exaggerated clothes. He struggled forward. "Underworld. Gangsters.

Well, you know what I mean! He tried to kill you. And you—well, naturally, sir—!"

The judge considered this.

"An inference," he replied, "both unwarranted and improper. Mr. Morell was my daughter's *fiancé*."

"Did you kill him, sir?"

"No."

The monosyllable was fashioned with care, and with finality. It almost finished Weems, who quite frankly did not know what to do. If it had been anyone except Mr. Justice Ireton, Weems would have cautioned him and taken him along to the station. But taking Mr. Justice Ireton to the police station would be like violating the law itself. You didn't do that to high-court judges, especially one whose eye froze you even now. Weems had begun to sweat. He wished to God the inspector were here: he wished it wasn't his responsibility.

In taking out his notebook, he fumbled it and dropped it on the floor. He told the judge about the interrupted 'phone call, while the judge looked dazed.

"Would you care to make a statement, sir? Tell me what happened, like?"

"No."

"You mean you won't?"

"Presently. Not now."

Weems seized at a hope. "Would you like to tell Inspector Graham, sir, if I ask you to come along to the police station and see him?"

"There," said Mr. Justice Ireton, making a slight gesture without unlacing the hands he had folded over his stomach, "is the telephone. Be good enough to 'phone Inspector Graham and ask him if he can come out here."

"But I can't touch that 'phone, sir! It's—"

"There is an extension in the kitchen out at the back. Use that."

"But, sir—!"

"Use it, please."

Weems felt as though someone had given him a push under the shoulder-blade. Mr. Justice Ireton did not move. His hands remained folded over his paunch. Yet he was as much master of the situation as though some other person had been found pistol in hand, over a dead body; and Mr. Justice Ireton surveyed it, dispassionately, from the bench. Weems did not argue: he went.

Frederick Barlow came into the room through the French window, his fists on his hips. If the judge was surprised to see him, he gave no sign; he merely watched while Barlow closed the door after Weems.

There were small, fine wrinkles round Barlow's eyes. The set of his jaw was aggressive when he looked steadily back at Mr. Justice Ireton, holding to the lapels of his old sports jacket and squaring himself as though for battle.

"You can get away with that sort of thing," Barlow observed as dispassionately as the judge, "with Weems. But not, I think, with Inspector Graham. Or with the Chief Constable."

"Perhaps not."

Barlow jerked his thumb towards the body of Anthony Morell, ugly in death. "Did you do it?"

"No."

"You're in a bad position. You realize that?"

"Am I? We shall see."

It was a flash of sheer vanity, all the more surprising because it came from Horace Ireton. Barlow was brought up with a bump against that calm arrogance; but it unnerved him, because he knew the dangers of it.

"What happened? You can tell *me*, at least."

"I don't know what happened."

"Oh, look here!"

"Kindly," said the judge, shielding his eyes with his hand, "moderate your tone when you speak to me. I do not know what happened. I did not even know the fellow was in the house."

He spoke without emotion, but his vivid little eyes moved round towards the closed door, and the palms of his hands moved slowly and softly on the arms of the chair: a gesture which told Barlow that his wits were very much awake.

"I expected Mr. Morell tonight," he went on, "on a matter of business."

"Yes?"

"But I was not aware that he had arrived. This is Saturday, Mrs. Drew's night off. I was in the kitchen, preparing my own dinner." His mouth moved with distaste. "It was at half past eight precisely. I was just opening a tin of asparagus—yes: the matter is funny, though you don't smile—when I heard a pistol shot and a sound presumably caused by the fall of the telephone. I came in here and found Mr. Morell as you see him. That's all."

"All?" echoed Barlow, with a sort of wild patience. "ALL?"

"Yes. All."

"But the revolver. What about that?"

"It was lying on the floor beside him. I picked it up. That was an error, I admit."

"Thank God you admit that much. You picked up the revolver and sat down in the chair there, and held it in your hand, for five minutes more?"

"Yes. I am only human. I was astounded by the irony of—"

"Of what?"

"Nothing."

Barlow has since said that he wondered then whether the old man had gone out of his mind. Every logical reason said that he had; yet instinct told Frederick Barlow that Mr. Justice Ireton had never been calmer or cooler than at that moment. It was something about the eyes, or the turn of the head. All the same, murder in a passion does queer things to the mental balance.

"It is murder, you know," Barlow pointed out.

"Obviously."

"Well! Committed by whom?"

"Presumably," returned the judge, "by anyone who wished to walk into an open house, through the front door or one of the French windows, and shoot Mr. Morell through the back of the head."

Barlow clenched his fists. "You'll allow me to act for you, of course."

"Indeed? Why should you act for me?"

"Because you don't seem to realize the seriousness of the position!"

"You underestimate my intelligence," said the judge, crossing his plump knees. "One moment. Let me remind you that before I was raised to the bench I had a criminal practice second only to that of my late friend Marshall Hall. If they know more tricks than I do, they deserve to hang me." He smiled slightly. "You don't believe a single word I say, do you?"

"I don't say that. But would *you* believe it, if you heard it from the bench?"

"Yes." The judge spoke simply. "I flatter myself that I am seldom wrong in taking a man's measure, or recognizing truth when I hear it."

"Still—"

"Then there is the question of motive. All law, as you should know yourself, is directed towards the question of motive. Is there any reason why I should have killed that unpresentable but inoffensive young man?"

This was the point at which Constance Ireton came into the room.

The judge seemed really startled. He passed his hand across his forehead, nor could he hide an expression of acute distress. Barlow thought: He loves her almost as much as I do, and that gleam of raw humanity is as revealing as the arrogance.

Constance had dried her eyes, though they were still reddish round the lids. Her look was one of stoical composure. The glance she directed towards the dead man had no emotion in it; nothing except a cold, steady dislike. She seemed forcing herself to look at him, to study him up and down, before she turned to her father.

"I didn't know you cared so much about me," she burst out—and was again on the edge of tears.

"What," asked the judge harshly, "are you doing here?"

Constance ignored this.

"He was nothing but a filthy…" She could not complete the sentence. She turned to Barlow and kept stabbing her finger towards the dead man. "He made Daddy promise to give him three thousand pounds if he gave me up.

"I listened, of course. Yesterday. When you were talking about me in here. Naturally! Who wouldn't? I sneaked up and listened; and first I was so shocked I couldn't believe my ears, and then I didn't know what to do. It was like having your heart cut out, listening to that."

She twisted her fingers together.

"I couldn't face it—at first. So I just smiled, and pretended. Tony didn't know to the minute he died that I knew. I laughed with him. And I went back to Taunton with him. And all the time I was thinking: When shall I get the courage to say, 'You filthy—'" She stopped. "Then I knew what I should do. I was going to wait until he saw Daddy tonight. And, just when he had his precious money almost in his hands, I was going to walk in and say, 'Don't pay him a penny; I know all about the swine.'"

Constance moistened her lips.

"Oh, that would have been wonderful!" Her voice rose, and she savoured triumph. "But I couldn't follow him today, because he went to London. He told me he was going to see his solicitor about our marriage arrangements. Smiling all the time, you see; and kissing me goodbye as though he couldn't get enough of me.

"And then—it went wrong again. I borrowed a car to get out here tonight, but it broke down. So I was late. It's all my fault. If I'd been here earlier, or if I'd spoken out yesterday, I could have prevented all this. I'm glad he's dead. He broke my heart: it may sound silly to say that, but he did! So I'm glad he's dead. But you shouldn't have done it; you *shouldn't*!"

Not a muscle moved in Mr. Justice Ireton's face.

"Constance," he said coldly and quietly, "do you want to get your father hanged?"

There was an empty pause, intensified by the girl's swift, scared look. She made a gesture as though she would clap her hand over her mouth; then she stood listening. They all listened. They heard nothing except the noise of the sea until the door-knob rattled, the door to the hall opened, and PC Weems softly returned.

CHAPTER VI

IF WEEMS HAD HEARD ANYTHING, HE GAVE NO SIGN OF it. His young, fresh-complexioned face was effulgent with a sense of duty done and responsibilities passed on.

"Inspector's on his way," he volunteered.

"Ah," murmured the judge.

"We've got to send all the way to Exeter for a fingerprint man and a photographer," said Weems. "So we can't touch anything yet. But I'm to look round, and make a sketch. And—" His eyes fell on Constance. He frowned. "Excuse me, miss. Haven't I seen you before?"

"That is my daughter, Constance."

"Oh? The young lady who was engaged to be married to—" Weems's uncertainty grew as he glanced at the dead man again. "Have *you* anything to tell me, miss?"

"No," said the judge.

"Sir, I've got my duty to do!"

Barlow intervened smoothly. "Which is, as Inspector Graham says," he suggested, "to look round. Particularly at that fellow's body. You know, constable, I think you might find something which we should probably miss."

Though far from satisfied, Weems considered this and nodded with some portentousness. He stalked across and focused his mind on the picture, stepping from one side to the other to get a better look. It gave Fred Barlow the opportunity to accompany him.

The wound in Morell's skull was clean, and there was no sign of powder-singeing. The revolver now on the chess table, an Ives-Grant ·32, looked about a size to have made that wound. On closer inspection, Barlow could see that Morell's hat, of pearl grey with an objectionable feather in it, had rolled under the desk. Beside it lay a crumpled handkerchief whose corner bore the initials AM. The mouthpiece of the telephone seemed to have been badly chipped by its fall.

"Don't touch him, sir!" Weems warned sharply.

"Soles of the shoes," said Barlow, indicating them, "damp and rather muddy. Suggesting (eh?) that he must have walked across that muddy lawn and through a window, rather than up the brick path to be admitted at the front door."

Weems was pinkly severe. "We don't know how he got in, sir, since Mr.—since his Lordship won't tell us. Mind you don't touch him, now." He broke off. "Lord Almighty!"

His jump was justified.

In his anxiety to keep Morell's body clear, Weems's own foot jolted the dead man's side. It was a large foot, just as Weems was so large a man that his helmet barely passed beneath the supercilious-looking moose's head affixed to the wall above the desk. Morell's grey coat had already been rucked and humped up round his shoulders. As the constable's foot kicked it, something that looked like thin bundles of paper slid softly from the tilted pocket, and spread out into three flimsy white packets.

Each packet contained ten banknotes of £100 denomination. Each was fastened round with a paper label of the City and Provincial Bank.

"Three thousand pounds!" said Weems, picking up one packet, and dropping it hastily. "Three thousand pounds!"

He saw that Constance's eyes had flashed towards her father; that Mr. Justice Ireton had taken a pair of spectacles out of his pocket, and was slowly swinging them by the stems; that Frederick Barlow looked anywhere but at the money. But he had no time to ask a question, for the front-door knocker began to rap sharply.

To the other three—who, each in his own way, was hardly breathing—that knocking sounded like a note of dread. To Weems it meant Inspector Graham, whom he hastened to admit.

Inspector Graham was large, red-faced, and subduedly genial. He had a pair of very vivid blue eyes, which contrasted with the pink-spotted face, the whites of the eyes, and the suspiciously white teeth when he laughed. At the moment he was not laughing; his geniality was only buttoned-up courtesy.

"Evening, sir," he said to the judge. His eyebrows went up. "Evening, miss." His eyebrows went up still further. "Evening, Mr. Barlow. Weems, you'd better wait in the passage."

"Yes, sir."

Graham, biting at his underlip, waited until Weems had gone. While he looked round the room, a sort of strawberry rash seemed to come and go on his face; they were later to know it as an indication of his moods. He addressed the judge heavily, but with deference, and warning.

"Now, sir, Weems told me over the 'phone what he found when he got here. I don't know what happened here; and I'm sure there must be an explanation, but"—here he looked very hard at Mr. Justice Ireton—"I'm bound to ask you to tell me about it."

"Willingly."

"Ah! Then," said Graham, producing his notebook, "who is this gentleman? The one who's been shot?"

"His name is Anthony Morell. He is, or was, engaged to be married to my daughter."

Graham looked up quickly.

"Is that so, sir? Congrat—I mean," the strawberry rash waxed rich, "I mean, very unfortunate and all! I hadn't heard Miss Ireton was engaged to be married."

"Nor had I, until yesterday."

Graham seemed taken aback.

"Yes. Well. What was Mr. Morell doing here tonight?"

"He was to have come to see me."

"*Was* to have come to see you, sir? I don't quite follow that."

"I mean that I did not see him tonight until after he was dead."

Slowly, with self-effacing quiet, Constance had moved over to sit down on the sofa. She pushed aside a gaudy sofa-cushion, adorned with the figure of a maple-leaf and the beaded inscription "Canada Forever," so that Barlow could sit down beside her. Instead he remained standing rigid, his greenish eyes now almost black with concentration. But she was trembling through all her body, so he dropped one hand on her shoulder. She was very grateful for it; it was warmth; and the sea-wind blew very cold.

Mr. Justice Ireton told his story.

"I see, sir. I see," rumbled Inspector Graham, in the tone of one who means, "I don't see at all." He cleared his throat. "And that's all you have to tell me, sir?"

"Yes."

As Graham echoed Frederick Barlow, so Mr. Justice Ireton merely echoed himself.

"I see. You were in the kitchen when you heard this shot?"

"Yes."

"And ran in here straight away?"

"Yes."

"How long afterwards, say?"

"Ten seconds."

"And found nobody here except Mr. Morell—dead?"

"That is so."

"Where was the revolver then, sir?"

Mr. Justice Ireton put on his spectacles, craned his neck round, and measured distances. "Lying on the floor beside the telephone, between the body and the desk."

"What did you do then?"

"I picked up the revolver and smelled the barrel, to see whether it had just been fired. And it had just been fired. That is for your information."

"But what I'm trying to get at, sir, is this," insisted Graham, with a set of his shoulders like one who is attempting to push a heavy motor car uphill. "*Why* did you pick up the gun? Didn't you of all people know that you're not supposed to do that? Come to think of it, I remember being in court once when you raised merry blazes with a witness just for picking up a knife by the tip."

Mr. Justice Ireton appeared perturbed.

"True," he said. "True," and ruffled the tips of his fingers across his forehead. "I had forgotten. The Mallaby case, wasn't it?"

"Yes, sir. You said—"

"One moment. I think I also pointed out to the jury, if you recall, that the action, though foolish and reprehensible, was a perfectly natural one. I know it was in my case. I could not help myself."

Inspector Graham went to the chess table and picked up the revolver. He sniffed at the fouled barrel. He broke it open, showing that one cartridge had been fired from an otherwise full magazine.

"Ever see this gun before, sir?"

"Not to my knowledge."

Graham glanced inquiringly at Constance and Barlow, both of whom shook their heads. Unspoken in all their minds, looming large and ominous in Graham's were the three packets of banknotes still lying on Morell's coat. You could almost follow the Inspector's thoughts: it was obvious that he did not like the dead man's foreign appearance.

"Sir," Graham went on, clearing his throat for the dozenth time, "let's go back to another matter. Why was Mr. Morell coming to see you tonight?"

"He wished to convince me that he would make an acceptable husband for my daughter."

"I don't follow that."

"Mr. Morell's real name," explained the judge, "was

Antonio Morelli. He figured in a case in Surrey five years ago, in which it was alleged that he tried to blackmail a wealthy girl into marriage, and she attempted to shoot him."

If somebody had pulled the handle of a slot-machine and rung up the jackpot, its result could not have been more apparent than the expression on Inspector Graham's face. You could almost see thoughts whirl and fall into line, with a click that released the hidden coins.

Fred Barlow said to himself: Is the old man scatty? Has he gone completely out of his mind? Yet a second later, only a trifle less quick than Mr. Justice Ireton himself, he realized the meaning of this. He remembered one of the judge's maxims, laid down to instruct a young lawyer. If you wish to gain a reputation for honesty, always answer with the utmost frankness any question, however damaging, to which an investigator can readily find out the answer for himself.

What was the old devil up to?

But Inspector Graham looked dazed.

"You admit that, sir?"

"Admit what?"

"That—that—" Graham, almost inarticulate, pointed towards the banknotes. "Well, that he asked money from you? And you gave it to him?"

"Certainly not."

"You didn't give him the money?"

"I did not."

"Then where did he get it?"

"I can't answer that question, Inspector. You should know better than to ask it."

Again, with sharp ominousness, the front-door knocker began to rap.

Graham held up his hand for silence, though nobody felt like speaking. They heard PC Weems's boots creak in the passage, and the opening of the front door. They heard the crisp middle-aged voice which spoke.

"I wish to see Mr. Anthony Morell."

"Yes, sir?" said Weems. "What name?"

"Appleby. I am Mr. Morell's solicitor. He instructed me to come to this address at eight o'clock tonight. Unfortunately I am not used to driving in your country lanes, and I lost my way." The voice broke off and suddenly sharpened, as though the speaker were peering in gloom. "Are you a policeman?"

"Yes, sir," said Weems. "This way."

Inspector Graham was at the door when Weems ushered in a middle-sized man with a brushed, precise manner. Mr. Appleby removed his bowler hat, and put it under the arm of the hand which held his briefcase. He wore gloves and an overcoat. What remained of Mr. Appleby's black hair was brushed straight across his skull from a wide parting. He had a hard mouth, a strong flat jaw, and shells of eyeglasses which magnified black, glistening, steady eyes.

Then Graham stood aside, so that he could see Morell's body. Mr. Appleby pushed out his lips like a fish, and they heard him draw in his breath. For perhaps five seconds he did not say anything. Then he spoke grimly.

"Yes," he said, and nodded. "Yes, I think I've come to the right address."

"Meaning what, sir?"

"Meaning that that is my client. There on the floor. Who are you?"

"I'm the local inspector of police. This is Mr. Justice Ireton's cottage; and that is Mr. Justice Ireton there." (Appleby ducked his head stiffly towards the judge, who did not return it.) "I'm here investigating the death of Mr. Morell, who was murdered here about half an hour ago."

"Murdered!" said Mr. Appleby. "Murdered!" He looked at the body. "At least I see he wasn't robbed."

"You mean that money there?"

"Naturally."

"You don't know who that money belonged to, do you, sir?"

Mr. Appleby's eyebrows travelled up a wrinkled forehead; even the thin hair on his scalp seemed to fold back. He was as much a picture of astonishment as his professional bearing allowed.

"Belonged to?" he repeated. "It belonged to Mr. Morell, of course."

In Constance Ireton, shrinking back on the sofa, there stirred one of those inspired guesses which can fly to the heart of confusion and find truth. She did not even guess: she knew. She felt her own heart contract; she felt a warmth flow from her waist up to her shoulders. Yet she had such difficulty in speaking that at first she could not force her voice through her lips.

"May I ask you something?" she cried: too loudly, and so unexpectedly that they all swung round. Then she corrected herself, though her voice remained husky. "May I ask you something?"

"Miss Ireton, I presume?" said Appleby.

"No, you're not to shut me up!" said Constance, looking instinctively at her father, and then back to Appleby with passion. "There's something I've got to know before we go any further. T-Tony always said he had lots and lots of money. What was he worth?"

"Worth?"

"How much money?"

Mr. Appleby looked rather shocked.

"How much money?" insisted Constance. (Please, dear God, make him tell me!)

"Times," said Appleby, "are not what they were. Business—er—is not what it was. But I should say—well, approximately—sixty thousand pounds."

"Sixty…thousand…pounds?" breathed Inspector Graham.

Mr. Justice Ireton was as white as a ghost. But only Fred Barlow noticed it.

"Mr. Morell, as you no doubt know," pursued Appleby, whether or not with veiled sarcasm could not be determined, "was owner and manager of Toni-Sweets Ltd. The firm manufactures toffees, chewing-gum, sweets of all kinds. Mr. Morell was not anxious to have his connection with it known, because he was afraid his friends would make fun of him."

The solicitor's jaw tightened.

"Frankly, I saw no reason for such delicacy. He had (heaven rest him) inherited a real business acumen from his Sicilian father. He started without a penny; and in less than four years he owned the present establishment. Of course—he had a reason for such drive. That money there, the three thousand pounds, he meant as a wedding-present for Miss Ireton."

"A wedding-present," said Constance.

Appleby spoke in clipped tones. A new, curious note had come into his voice; emotionless, yet, to an attentive ear, significant.

"He came to me in London today with an odd story which I don't understand even yet. No matter! He wanted me to come here tonight and present a statement of his financial position. 'Slapping the money on the table,' he called it."

Inspector Graham whistled.

"Is that so, now? To prove he wasn't—?"

Appleby ignored this, smiling a dreary smile which nevertheless had pity in it.

"He also wanted me to assure Mr. Justice Ireton that he would make a suitable husband for Miss Ireton. That's hardly in my line. And it's hardly necessary now. But I tell you so for what it's worth.

"Mr. Morell had his faults. They were chiefly those of bad taste and—well, a certain vindictiveness. Basically he was conscientious, hard-working, and (may I say?) very much in love with Miss Ireton. He would have made a good family man after the fashion of the *petit bourgeois* stock he sprang from. Unfortunately—"

Making a gesture towards Morell's body, Appleby slapped the briefcase against his leg and lifted his shoulders. He added:

"I am sorry to distress you, Miss Ireton."

For a second Barlow thought she was going to faint. She was leaning back against the sofa holding tightly to a pillow, her eyes closed. The muscles moved up and down in her throat. Yet, even as his heart went out to her, Fred Barlow glanced at Mr. Justice Ireton.

The judge still sat motionless, though he had taken off his spectacles and was swinging them back and forth. A small bead of sweat appeared on his smooth forehead. Barlow did not look at his eyes. Yet among the confused emotions Barlow felt then, admiration, friendship, pain, pity, and guilty gladness that Morell was dead, one small thought wormed through everything and prevailed above all:

The bloody fool. He's killed the wrong man.

CHAPTER VII

AT ABOUT NINE O'CLOCK ON THAT SAME NIGHT, MISS Jane Tennant drove her car into the car park beside the Esplanade Hotel, Tawnish.

The Esplanade is a showplace, garish between the skeins of lights along the promenade and the red hills behind. Its famous basement swimming-pool, with tea and cocktail lounge attached, offered the luxury of warmed sea water in winter—and on such summer days, which were many, when only an Eskimo could have ventured into the sea without triple pneumonia. Jane Tennant was to remember that swimming-pool in the future.

At the moment she merely entered the hotel and asked at the desk for Dr. Gideon Fell. It was out of season, and there were not many guests despite the crowd of transients along the promenade. She was informed that, though Dr. Fell had not the remotest notion who Miss Tennant might be, he was very pleased to see anyone at any time; and would she come up to his room?

She found Dr. Fell in a large over-decorated room on the second floor. Dr. Fell wore slippers and a purple dressing-gown as big as a tent. He was sitting at the table before a portable typewriter, with a pint of beer at his elbow, tapping out notes.

"You don't know me," said Jane Tennant. "But I know all about you."

In his turn he saw a girl perhaps twenty-eight or twenty-nine years old. She was very attractive, though not pretty; somewhat large-boned, though not large; quiet, though by nature inclined to talk. The combination is difficult to describe, though not so difficult to analyse.

Her best feature was her fine figure, of which she perhaps did not make the most. Her eyes were good, too—grey eyes, with pin-point black pupils. Her dark brown hair was bobbed, her mouth large. She wore country tweeds, which did not do justice to her well-developed figure, with brown stockings and flat-heeled shoes. And she breathed as though she had been running.

Supporting himself on his crutch-headed stick, Dr. Fell surged up to welcome her, almost upsetting the typewriter, the notes, and the beer. He made quite a ceremony of installing her in a chair. For he liked the look of Jane Tennant. He sensed about her an intelligence, a quiet gleam of mirth which was not apparent now.

"A pleasure," beamed the doctor, still somewhat foggy from note-taking. "A pleasure. Er—will you have a pint of beer?"

He was surprised and delighted when she accepted.

"Dr. Fell," she said simply, "has a total stranger ever come to you and confided her troubles?"

The doctor wheezed back into his seat.

"Often," he answered, with the utmost seriousness.

Jane looked at the floor, and spoke rapidly. "I ought to explain that I know Marjorie Wills—Marjorie Elliot, her name is now. You got her out of awfully bad trouble in the Sodbury Cross poisoning case; and she rather raves about you. Then last night Connie Ireton (that's the judge's daughter) mentioned that you were staying hereabouts, and said she'd met you at her father's bungalow."

"Yes?"

"Well," said the girl, smiling a little, "would you mind if a total stranger—did it now?"

For answer Dr. Fell gathered up his papers, shuffled them, and shut them away in the drawer of the table. He also attempted to put the cover on the portable typewriter. But, as this is a process at which fingers turn to doughy thumbs and can seldom be managed even with the aid of bangings and profanity, it did not succeed until Jane Tennant took the cover from him and with brisk, capable fingers clicked it into place.

"One day," observed Dr. Fell, "I shall beat that swine and muzzle him at the first go. Meanwhile, I am all attention."

But the girl only looked at him helplessly, while seconds lengthened into a minute.

"I don't know how to begin. I can't *say* it!"

"Why not?"

"Oh, I haven't committed a crime or anything like that. It's just a question of what I ought to do. But saying it—well, I'm afraid I'm not enough of an exhibitionist."

"Try," suggested Dr. Fell, "stating it as a hypothetical case. You'll feel better."

There was a pause.

"All right," nodded Jane, looking at the floor. "A certain woman whom we'll call X is in love with…" She raised her head, and her eyes grew defensive. "I suppose all this sounds very petty and foolish to you?"

"No, by thunder but it doesn't!" returned Dr. Fell, with such obvious sincerity that she drew a deep breath through her full breast, and tried again.

"A certain woman whom we'll call X is in love with a lawyer—no, say just a man—"

"Say a lawyer. It removes the algebra while preserving the anonymity."

Again he saw under the repressed exterior that hidden gleam of mirth. But she only nodded.

"If you like. A lawyer whom we'll call Y. But Y is gone on, or thinks he is gone on, another girl: say Z. Z is very pretty: X isn't. Z is very young; X is on thirty. Z is lively; X isn't." A shadow crossed her face. "*That's* all right. The problem enters when Z falls for, and becomes engaged to a man whom we'll simply designate as Casanova."

Dr. Fell inclined his head gravely.

"And that's the trouble. Now, X is convinced that Y is not in love with this little blonde, and never has been. He doesn't *need* a girl like that. X is convinced, on her word of honour, that if the little blonde marries her Casanova, then Y will forget her in a month. She'll be out of his life. The hypnosis will be over. Then perhaps Y will see—"

"I understand," said Dr. Fell.

"Thanks." It was physical anguish for her to tell this story; tension seemed to be released all through her. "Consequently,

X should be cheering for this match. She should want to see the happy couple wedded and bedded as soon as possible. Shouldn't she?"

"Yes."

"Yes. Then Fr—then Y would be able to see that there's somebody else who's rather fond of him. Who adores him, rather. Who would be content just to sit and listen to him talk. Who—well, there it is!"

Again Dr. Fell inclined his head.

"Unfortunately," continued Jane, "X happens to know something about this man Casanova. She happens to know that he's a nasty bit of work who ought to be exposed. She happens to know that he's a crooked gigolo who was mixed up in a nasty scandal at Reigate five years ago. And she's sure of this because she knows the inner facts of that case, which didn't come out at the trial and which would make any girl, no matter how infatuated, wake up with a bang if she heard them."

It is not possible for a man of Dr. Fell's dimensions to give a start, except one which might be measured by a seismograph. But he almost managed it when he heard of the Reigate affair. His face grew more fiery, and he puffed behind his bandit's moustache so that the black ribbon on his eyeglasses blew wildly.

Jane was not watching him.

"I'm afraid I can't keep up this algebra pretence any longer," she said. "You don't have to be Gideon Fell to guess that X is me. Y is Fred Barlow. Z is Connie Ireton. And Casanova is Antonio Morelli, alias Anthony Morell."

There was a long silence, broken only by Dr. Fell's wheezing breaths.

"The point is," Jane muttered, "what am I to *do*? I know men think all women are predatory beasts of the jungle. You think we'd see each other torn to pieces like winking. But it's not true. I'm fond of Connie. Very fond. If I let her marry that—that—

"But suppose I tell her, and bring Cynthia Lee down to prove it? Whether she believed me or not, she'd only hate me. Fred Barlow would hate me too, probably. Out of pity, it would only draw him closer to her. I could tell the judge on the q.t., of course, but that would be sheer sneaking; and, anyway, it would have the same effect on Fred. Ever since they came down to my house-party last Wednesday, and I recognized 'Tony Morell,' I've been battering my brains to think of a way out. I don't want to treat you like Aunt Hester's Department for the Lovelorn, but what am I to *do*?"

Dr. Fell drew the air through one nostril with a vast, puzzled, and lion-like inhalation.

He shook his head. Hoisting himself to his feet, he lumbered up and down the room in his old purple dressing-gown, making the chandelier rattle. His face wore more of an expression of gargantuan distress than even Jane Tennant's story would seem to warrant. Even the arrival of a waiter, with a pint of beer for which he had rung five minutes ago, could not rouse him. Both he and Jane looked at the beer as though they could not imagine what it was.

"The matter," he conceded, when the waiter had gone, "is difficult. Harrumph. Very difficult."

"Yes. *I* think so."

"The more so as—" He stopped short. "Tell me. When

Morell came to your house-party on Wednesday, did he recognize you?"

Jane frowned.

"Recognize me? He's never seen me in his life."

"But you said—"

"Oh!" For some reason she seemed relieved. "I should have explained that I never knew him personally. Cynthia Lee, the girl he got in with, was my friend at school. While all this was going on, she used to come to my flat in Town, and have hysterics, and tell me all about it. I'm supposed to be a good listener." Jane made a grimace with her lips. "But I wasn't concerned in the business, so I never appeared in it."

"You may consider it irrelevant," grunted Dr. Fell, eyeing her, "if I ask you to tell me just a little more about Morell and Cynthia Lee. Believe me, I have a reason."

Jane looked puzzled.

"Do you know anything about the case?"

"H'mf, yes. A little."

"Well, when he threatened to show her letters to her father unless she married him, Cynthia got a gun and tried to kill him. She shot him in the leg."

"Yes?"

"The police didn't want to prosecute. But Morell, that vindictive little devil, insisted on his rights, and they had to. He wanted to see Cynthia go to jail. The defence was faked, of course. That made our Mr. Morell wild. The prosecution couldn't even produce the revolver Cynthia had used. The best they could do was to produce a box of cartridges of a sort that would fit the revolver, and show they found the box in Cynthia's house. Of course the jury must have guessed the defence was a fake; everybody in court did. But they calmly returned a verdict of not guilty. That made Morell even wilder."

Jane's lip curled. She had almost shaken off the heavy restraint which characterized her.

"There was a dreadful scene in court when the verdict was brought in. Morell was sitting at the solicitors' table. He's got a sort of Dago dramatic sense—like a crude Borgia. The box of cartridges, as an exhibit, was beside him. He picked one of the bullets out of that box, and held it up, and shouted, 'I'm going to keep this as a reminder that there's no justice in England. Now I'm going to make my way in the world; and, when I do, it'll remind me to tell you what I think of all of you.'"

"And then?"

"The judge, Mr. Justice Wythe, told him to shut his head or he'd be committed for contempt of court."

Jane smiled a little, though not from amusement. Seeing the tankard of beer, she picked it up and drank.

"The county rallied round Cynthia nobly. Shall I tell you something that not two or three other people in the world know?"

"Any human being," said Dr. Fell, "is always pleased to get a bit of information like that."

"Did you ever hear of Sir Charles Hawley?"

"Who has since," said Dr. Fell, "been raised to the bench as Mr. Justice Hawley?"

"Yes. He was an eminent barrister then; he defended Cynthia. He was a great friend of Cynthia's family, and he *pinched* that revolver I was telling you about, to show he was in as deeply as anybody else. It's a fact. He hid it in his own

house, I'd seen it any number of times: it was an Ives-Grant
·32, with a little cross cut with a penknife in the steel under
the magazine-chamber. Oh, Lord, I'm talking too much!"

Dr. Fell shook his head.

"No," he replied seriously, "I don't think you are. You said
a moment ago that there were things that didn't come out at
the trial. What things?"

Jane hesitated, but Dr. Fell's eye remained fixed.

"Well…that Cynthia had been forging cheques in her
father's name to give Morell a monthly allowance."

There was such concentrated contempt in her tone that
Dr. Fell decided to probe still further. She lifted the tankard
and drank again.

"I gather you can't imagine any woman doing that?" the
doctor suggested.

"That? Oh, no. Not a bit of it. I might do it myself. But not
for Morell, you see. Not for a thing like *Morell*."

"Still, Miss Lee must have been rather fond of him?"

"She was, poor kid."

"Where is she now, do you know?"

The grey eyes clouded. "Oddly enough, she lives not far
from here. In a private sanatorium. She's not—you know!—
but she's always been neurotic and that affair didn't help her.
Tony Morell knew she was neurotic when he took up with her.
That's another of the things that shall not be forgiven him.
If I were to bring her here and show her to Connie Ireton…
You see what I mean?"

"I do."

Shaking her full shoulders, Jane lifted the tankard and
drank again. "Well?" she prompted.

"I suggest that you leave the matter to me."

Jane sat up. "You mean that?—But to do what?"

"Frankly, I don't know yet," admitted the doctor, spreading out his hands and speaking with fiery argumentativeness. "You see, I have known Horace Ireton for a long time, though I can't say I've been exactly a close friend of his. His daughter I met yesterday. I don't necessarily maintain we should have another Cynthia Lee on our hands in case of a smash, but—Archons of Athens! I don't like it."

"No friend of Connie's *would* like it."

"Then there is yourself, Miss X," said Dr. Fell, colouring up guiltily, "to whom I have—harrumph!—rather taken a fancy. We must consider you too. Just one more point." His face grew grave. "You give me your word that all this inside information about Morell is strictly true?"

For answer the girl reached down and took up a brown leather handbag from the floor beside her chair. Fishing out a gold pencil, she scribbled some words on the sheet of an address book, tore out the sheet, and handed it across to Dr. Fell.

"'Sir Charles Hawley,'" he read, "'18 Villiers Mansions, Cleveland Row, London, S.W.1.'"

"Ask him," Jane advised simply. "If you catch him after lunch he'll tell you all about it. Except the revolver, of course; he'll never mention that. Only for heaven's sake don't let on I was the one who sent you."

On a bedside table in an alcove of the big room, the telephone rang.

"Excuse me," said Dr. Fell.

On the mantelpiece there was an ornate marble clock

whose little pendulum switched back and forth with steady ticking. Its hands pointed to twenty-five minutes past nine.

Jane Tennant did not look at it. While Dr. Fell lumbered over to the shrilling 'phone, she drew a compact out of her handbag and studied the reflection of her face in its mirror. Her hard breathing had slowed down long ago, but she still seemed to be asking herself fiercely whether she had done the right thing.

She turned her face from side to side as she looked into the mirror, she made a grimace. Jane wore no lipstick and very little powder; hers was the complexion of full-blooded health, which redeemed the rather plain face. Instead of adding anything, she took out a comb and drew it through her thick, wiry brown hair. Her look was now one of intense bitterness. Below, from the promenade, the shuffle of a crowd boiled up against these windows.

"Hello?" roared Dr. Fell, who is usually incomprehensible on the telephone. "Who?... Graham... Ah! How are you, Inspector?... *Eh?*"

His exclamation was so thunderous that Jane involuntarily glanced round.

Dr. Fell's mouth was partly open, making the moustache droop. His eyes, unseeing, were fixed on her. She could hear a thin voice chattering on the receiver.

Her lips sketched: "What is it?"

Dr. Fell put his hand over the mouthpiece of the 'phone.

"Tony Morell has been murdered," he said.

For a space while you might have counted ten, Jane Tennant sat motionless, the compact as though paralysed in her fingers. Then she dropped it into the handbag, snapped shut the catch, and sprang to her feet with an animal-like litheness. If emotion had been sound, the room would have been full of a wash like the noise of the sea. But there was only the clock, and Dr. Fell's voice.

"Ireton's bungalow… About an hour ago." His eyes strayed to the clock. "Tut, man, nonsense!"

Jane Tennant's ears hurt with the pain of listening when she tried to catch that other voice.

"Oh? With what make of revolver…?"

"What calibre…?"

As he heard the reply, Dr. Fell's eyes widened and then narrowed behind the eyeglasses on the black ribbon. It was as though a dull, only half-incredible idea had occurred to him while he stared back at Jane Tennant.

"Is that so, hey?" His voice was elaborately casual. "No distinguishing marks on the revolver, I suppose?"

The telephone answered at length.

"I see," grunted the doctor. "No. No, I don't mind lending a hand. 'Bye."

He replaced the receiver. Lowering his head so that several chins folded over his collar, he leaned both hands on his crutch-headed stick, and stood for a moment winking and blinking incredulously at the floor.

CHAPTER VIII

IN THE LIVING-ROOM OF MR. JUSTICE IRETON'S BUNGA-low Mr. Herman Appleby was contemplating the effects of the hand-grenade he had just flung among his listeners.

"But of course," the solicitor added, "you were aware of all this? That is to say: you knew Mr. Morell was a wealthy man, as wealthy men are counted these days?"

Appleby looked at the judge, who inclined his head.

"I did," assented Mr. Justice Ireton.

Inspector Graham drew a powerful breath of relief.

"To be more exact," the judge corrected himself, in a cold and careful voice, "that was what Mr. Morell said his position was. He was to come here tonight to prove it to my satisfaction, and over his suggested wedding-gift of three thousand pounds. Er—I forget whether I had already told you that, Inspector?"

Graham nodded.

"You did, sir!" he assured them all. "You certainly did! I remember it now."

"Ah. You might just write it down again, in case you are uncertain. Thank you... Mr. Barlow!"

"Sir?"

"My daughter seems to be unwell. I should prefer not to have her exposed to this unpleasant business any more than is necessary. You agree, Inspector? Mr. Barlow, will you be good enough to take her into the other room; and, when she has sufficiently recovered, drive her home?"

Fred Barlow held out his hand to Constance. After a hesitation she took it.

He was glad that he had his back to the others, for they were now moving through the most dangerous emotional phase yet. The source of potential danger was Constance. If she let herself go, in any way whatever, not even the judge's arrogant self-assurance could carry the lie much further.

Constance, her eyes looking brown and burned and deep-set, her makeup like a clown's paint on a beautiful face, opened her mouth to speak. Barlow glared a warning. A spark flicked the powder-train and went out. She took his extended hand, and pulled herself up from the sofa. Silently, with Barlow's arm round her shoulder, they went out of the room. But in the hall the other three heard her burst into hysterical sobs.

Mr. Justice Ireton blinked rapidly, several times.

"You will excuse me, gentlemen," he said. "I do not go into this without pain."

Inspector Graham coughed, and Appleby bowed stiffly.

"However! Go into it we must," continued the judge. "In what I have said, I think this gentleman should be able to confirm me. You, sir. Mr.—?"

"Appleby."

"Ah, yes. Appleby. May I ask what Mr. Morell said when he called on you today?"

Appleby considered. Behind that professional mask of his, Inspector Graham (who was nobody's fool) had an uncertain impression that the solicitor was laughing. Graham did not know why he felt this. From his scanty but well-brushed hair to his perhaps scanty but well-brushed morals nothing could have been more correct than the solicitor's bearing.

"Said? Let me see. He said that he was playing a game on Mr. Justice Ireton—"

"Game?" interposed Graham sharply.

"—which he promised to explain later. What he meant I can't say. I have had the pleasure of seeing you many times in court, sir."

The judge's eyebrows went up, but he merely inclined his head in acknowledgement.

"One other thing!" said Appleby, reflecting. "He made the remark, rather odd, that you yourself had fixed the amount of Miss Ireton's wedding-present. He said he had tried to persuade you to go higher; but you refused."

"Indeed. And why is that so odd?"

"Well…"

"Why is it so odd, Mr. Appleby? Surely three thousand pounds may be considered generous enough?"

"I don't say it isn't. I only—let it go, let it go!" The solicitor made a gesture, and brushed a grain of sand from his overcoat with a gloved hand.

"He said nothing else?"

"Nothing. And now, in the interests of my late client, may

I ask a question? Have you any idea who killed him? What, precisely, happened here? I submit I've a right to know that."

Inspector Graham eyed him.

"Well, sir, we were hoping you could help us there."

"*I* could? Why so?"

"Knowing him, and all. You did know him pretty well, I imagine?"

"Yes, in a way."

"He wasn't robbed," Graham pointed out. "That's certain, if nothing else is. Did he have enemies, for instance?"

Appleby hesitated. "Yes, he did. I can't tell you anything about his private life. He had one or two bad business enemies." Surprisingly, Appleby seemed to consider this point with more care than any of the others. With a word of apology he put down his briefcase and his bowler hat on the chess table, and thrust his hands into the pockets of his overcoat.

"I told you the poor fellow was a queer mixture," he went on. "He could be generous enough. *Vide* that money. But, if he thought anybody had done him a slight or an injury he would devise the most elaborate and Machiavellian schemes to get level." Appleby glanced at the judge. "You understand that, of course, sir."

"How should I understand it?"

Appleby laughed.

"Don't misunderstand. I'm not speaking personally! After all, a gift like that to Miss Ireton could hardly be called doing you an injury." His glance was meaning. "No: I meant you could understand the workings of a mind like that, from your great experience on the bench."

"Perhaps."

"Then, too, there was his business drive. He had an unfortunate love-affair about five years ago—"

"You mean," interrupted Graham, "when he tried to blackmail the young lady, and she shot him?"

Appleby seemed taken aback. But he spoke softly.

"There was something to be said for the boy too, you know."

"I never heard it," snapped Graham. "You don't think the young lady'd be still holding a grudge, now?"

"I know almost nothing about the affair. That is your province, Inspector."

"But these business enemies of Mr. Morell's?"

"You must excuse me from talking slander," Appleby said with decision. "If you read through his business files, as you probably will, you'll find names and suggestions which you can interpret as you like. That's the most I can tell you."

Graham was looking more and more worried, as though each person and situation turned into a new greased pig which he could not hold.

"*You* knew he was coming here tonight, sir. Do you know if he told anybody else?"

"I can't say. He probably did. He wasn't one to guard his tongue, except when he had something up his sleeve."

"But think, sir. Isn't there *anything* more you can tell me that would help?"

Appleby was thoughtful. "No, I don't believe so. As he was leaving my office I said, 'If we're both going down there tonight, why don't we go together? Let me give you a lift in my car.' He said, 'No. I want to see Mr. Ireton before you do. I'm taking the 4.5 train, which will get me into Tawnish at just on eight o'clock. Perhaps I'll even meet him in the train. He said he'd be in town today.'—If that helps any?"

Graham swung round to the judge.

"Oh? You were in London today, sir?"

"Yes."

"May I ask what you were doing there?"

A shade of weary exasperation passed over Mr. Justice Ireton's large, smooth forehead.

"I usually go up on Saturdays, Inspector."

"Yes, sir; but—"

"Confound it all! I made a few purchases, and looked in at my club. But I hadn't the pleasure of seeing Mr. Morell on the train. I had an early lunch with my old friend Sir Charles Hawley. After that I took the 2.15 to Tawnish, and a taxi from the station to here."

Drawing a deep breath, Graham returned to the solicitor.

"Just one other thing, Mr. Appleby. That revolver on the table there, beside your briefcase: did you ever see it before? Yes, you can handle it if you want to!"

Appleby treated the question with his usual meticulous care. He picked up the weapon in his gloved hands, stepped under the central chandelier, and turned the revolver over and over.

"No, I can't say I do. One of these things looks very much like another." He peered up. "The number's been filed off, I notice. Evidently a long time ago."

"Yes, sir," said Graham dryly. "We noticed that too. It didn't belong to Mr. Morell himself, did it?"

Appleby looked startled.

"That's an odd idea! I don't know, but I shouldn't think it was likely. He hated firearms. He—"

"Hold on, sir!" interrupted Graham sharply.

The solicitor, his shells of eyeglasses opaque-glittering under the four-bulb chandelier, started and lifted one shoulder higher than the other. His expression was one of surprise underlaid by some other emotion.

But Graham spoke in no tone of menace. As the Ives-Grant ·32 was held tilted under the light, Graham's eye caught something he had not previously seen. He took the weapon out of Appleby's hands and studied it. On one side of it, just under the cartridge-drum, someone had cut into the steel a small figure like a cross: the horizontal arm short, the vertical bar long.

"Like a religious cross," he decided. "Might be useful."

"Or," said Mr. Justice Ireton placidly, "it might not."

None of them saw the handle of the door move, or heard the latch click shut. Fred Barlow, who had been listening outside in the passage, moved quietly across to the bedroom.

There were no lights in this passage. The front door stood open. Outside, where the sky had cleared into a night of big unsteady stars, Barlow could see PC Weems pacing up and down the flagged path to the gate.

The judge's bedroom was dark, too, for Constance had turned out the light. The big, heavy bedroom furniture— which had belonged to the bungalow's late owner, Mr. Johnson of Ottawa—made shadows against starlight through the front windows. Barlow could discern a patch of white where Constance sat huddled in a rocking-chair beside the middle window. Constance was sobbing: sniffling, rather: and she cried peevishly to him to go away.

"No, don't go," she added, swinging back and forth in the rocking-chair so that it squeaked. "Come here. I'm so miserable I could die."

He put his hand on her shoulder in the gloom.

"I know. I'm sorry."

"You're not sorry," said Constance, shaking off the hand. "You detested him."

"I only met him once, Connie."

"You detested him! You know you detested him!"

Somewhere inside him, Barlow felt a pang of what he recognized as disappointment. Of all things, he thought, he oughtn't to feel disappointment. Constance had been through agony, of two kinds, twice sending her to opposite extremes.

Yet there it was. He experienced again the feeling that had been haunting and baffling him for several years: a groping, a feeling of something missing, a sense of life not quite fulfilled. Frederick Barlow was not an introspective person. Except for the one black spot in his mind, the one recent sudden thing he must not think about, he took the world as he found it. Still...

"All right," Barlow said, "I detested him. You're better off without him, Connie."

"He was worth two of you!"

"He may have been. Admitted. I still say you're better off without him."

Constance's mood changed.

"He was a silly, stupid fool," she cried, making the rocker squeak violently. "Why couldn't he have said he had all that money? Why couldn't he have come to Daddy and *said* so? Why did he let Daddy (and me!) think he was a... Fred?"

"Yes?"

"Do you think Daddy killed him?"

"Sh-h!"

The three French windows, as in the living-room, had white net coverings which could hardly be called curtains, and which made only a shadowy mesh against the starlight.

Putting his face against the curtain, Barlow could see PC Weems still pacing the path, and hear the faint rasp of his footsteps. Constance spoke in a frightened whisper.

"They can't hear us, can they?"

"Not if you keep your voice down."

"Well? Do you think Daddy did it?"

"Listen, Connie. Do you trust me?"

Her eyes opened wide in the gloom. "Naturally," she said.

"Then do you realize"—he spoke softly but distinctly—"that it's only the sheer force of the old man's personality, his godlike assumption that what he says must be accepted, which keeps him from being under arrest this minute? Do you?"

"I—"

"He hypnotized the constable. He's half hypnotized Graham. For the moment, thank the Lord, he's had a bit of luck. I mean the news about Morell's unsuspected wealth. And you saw him instantly grab it and play it for all it was worth. I can't help admiring the way he whizzes over thin ice without batting an eyelid. He can say to Graham: 'I'm not a rich man, and I live above my income. Is it reasonable to suppose I should have shot the faithful suitor who can give my daughter all the luxury she wants?'"

Constance's eyes overflowed again, and she began to rock with hysterical vigour.

"I'm sorry. I'm sorry! But you've got to understand this,

so that you can be steady enough to help him by confirming what he says."

"Then you do think Daddy did it!"

"I think they may arrest him. Mind, I say *may*. Once they start to examine that story of his, about his being in the kitchen opening a tin of asparagus while Morell was shot in the front room, there's likely to be trouble. Don't you see the flaws in it?" He spoke drearily. "No, I don't suppose you do."

"I'm not c-clever like some people."

"Don't let's quarrel, Connie."

"Go away from me! You're deserting him too."

"Far from it," said Barlow, with more vehemence than he meant to show. He leaned one knee on the edge of the rocking-chair, stilling its movement. He took hold of its arms, and bent over Constance. He felt, under the high incurious stars, that he had to explain how one atom felt.

"Listen to me. Your father and I have always been at opposite ends of interpreting the legal code. He's a great man. He's taught me more than I ever hoped to learn. But he can't teach me to despise the beaten, the crippled, the under-dog, the man who can't fight because he has no education and can't explain because there are no words. Like Lypiatt. Do you remember Lypiatt's face, when sentence was pronounced?"

He felt her body grow tense, and heard the ticking of the watch on her wrist.

"Connie, I hate the smugness of the just. I hate their untroubled eyes. I hate their dictum, which is: 'This man's motives do not count. He stole because he was hungry or killed because he was driven past the breaking point, and therefore he shall be convicted.' I want a fair fight to win my case and say: 'This man's motives do count. He stole because he was hungry or killed because he was driven past the breaking point; and therefore, by God, he shall go free.'"

"Fred Barlow," said Constance, "what on earth are you talking about?"

He released his knee from the rocking-chair, and stood up. Her common-sense directness, like a pail of cold water, always made him feel ashamed of himself. As a rule he had himself well in hand. Now the night mocked him.

"Sorry," he said in his customary voice, and laughed. "This thing is making us all a little emotional. I was just having my go, that's all."

"But what do you *mean*?"

"I mean I want to help your father. What I'm afraid of is that he won't accept anybody's help; and, believe me, Connie, that's bad."

"Why?"

"Because he thinks he can't make a mistake."

There was a flash of lamps in the road outside, and a car drew up outside the gate of the bungalow. Seeing a hump against the sky, he guessed that this must be the photographer and fingerprint man from Exeter. He peered at the luminous dial of Constance's wrist-watch, and noted that the hour was nearly twenty-five minutes past nine.

"What you've got to do, my dear—is this clear?—is to hold tight to your nerves and back up his story that you knew Morell was well off. That's your job; and mind you do it properly, or you won't be your father's daughter. Now listen, and I'll tell you what else you've got to say."

While he coached her, speaking firmly and making sure

she understood, the rocking-chair creaked back and forth. But when she spoke for herself her voice was small, and painful in its appeal.

"You haven't answered my question, Fred. Do you think Daddy did it?"

"Frankly, I can't make up my mind."

Again the chair creaked.

"Fred!"

"Yes?"

"I know Daddy did it."

CHAPTER IX

WHILE HE STARED BACK AT HER IN THE GLOOM, SHE kept nodding her head witlessly, like a china figure.

"You don't mean you saw—?"

"Yes," said Constance.

He motioned her to silence. The newcomers outside, after a word with PC Weems, were tramping up the flagged path. Barlow groped across the bedroom and opened the door to the hall. Across the passage he could see light from the living-room, whose door stood ajar. From it issued Inspector Graham's heavy voice.

"Then we needn't delay you any longer, Mr. Appleby. You can go back to London, but leave your address."

An indistinguishable mutter.

"No! For the last time, you *cannot* take the banknotes! I admit it's a large sum; I admit it belongs to Mr. Morell's estate; but it's part of our evidence and I'm bound to keep it. Rest assured we'll take good care of it. *Good* night, sir!—Ah, boys, come in!"

A sullen-scowling Appleby, fitting on his bowler hat, shouldered out past the two uniformed men who had just arrived.

"First off, see if there are any prints on that telephone," Graham instructed. "As soon as you do, I want to ring up a friend of mine at the Esplanade." His voice altered as though he had swung round. "You agree it might be a good idea to ring Dr. Fell, sir?"

"If you like," conceded the judge's voice. "Though he's a very bad chess player."

Barlow's skin crawled, with something like a premonition of disaster, as he caught the undertone of Mr. Justice Ireton's voice. It was an undertone of contempt.

He shut the door and returned to Constance.

"Tell me," he muttered.

"There's nothing to tell. I saw Tony arrive here."

"You mean you met him?"

"No, dear. I saw him."

"When was this?"

"About twenty-five minutes past eight, near enough."

"What happened?"

"Well, Tony came along the road, chewing gum and muttering to himself and looking like fire. I was almost close enough to touch him, but he never noticed me."

"Where were you then?"

"I was—I was coupied down beside the fence, out in front."

"What the devil for?"

"So Tony shouldn't see me." Constance's tone was a mixture of anger, defensiveness, and fear. "You see, the car I borrowed went wonky up by Horseshoe Bay, in the other direction from Tawnish: near where your cottage is. It ran out of petrol, really."

"Yes?"

"I thought of going to your place and asking for a lift. But I didn't want you to know anything about it, the way I was feeling. So I walked along the road. When I was nearly to the gate I heard Tony coming. There's a lamp a little way down and I could see him plainly. I didn't want him to see me. I wanted him to get inside with Daddy, for—for sort of moral support, before I told him what I thought of him. You do understand, don't you?"

"I think so. Go on."

Her thin voice shook.

"Tony opened the gate, and went in, and cut diagonally across the lawn to the French windows of the living-room. He opened one and went in. Why are you making a face like that?"

"Because, as far as it goes, it confirms your father's story. Good!"

Constance folded her arms as though she were cold. "Come to think of it—it does, doesn't it?"

"Go on: what happened then?"

"I don't know. Oh, except that somebody turned on the lights."

"Weren't they on before?"

"Only that little desk lamp with the metal shade. The chandelier lights weren't on until then. I didn't want to go up there yet. So I went across the road and down over the bank towards the beach, and sat there below the road on the edge of the beach, feeling horribly miserable. I was still sitting there when I heard the—you know—bang. I guessed what it was. I'm not such a fool as you think."

"What did you do then?"

"I sat there for maybe a minute or two, frightened out of my wits. After that I sort of scrambled up the bank, and got my shoes full of sand, and started for the bungalow."

Barlow sorted out his thoughts. "Stop a bit," he said. "While you were down there on the other side of the bank, could you see the bungalow?"

"No. Naturally not."

"So somebody *could* have followed Morell in, and shot him, and got out again, without your seeing him?"

"Yes, I suppose so."

"Great, suffering...! No; go on!"

"Fred, I sneaked up the lawn and took a quick look through the window. There was Tony on the floor, just as you saw him. There was Daddy sitting in the same chair, with the revolver in his hand, just as you saw him a few minutes later. Only he looked much, much more scared then than he did when you and the policeman went in. That's all."

There was a long silence.

Barlow fished in the pockets of his baggy sports coat after cigarettes and matches. He found one, and lit it. The match flame was reflected in the window panes; it illuminated his green, watchful, puzzled eyes, etching the fine wrinkles round them and in comma marks round his mouth. Momentarily it brought Constance's face out of the dark, the chin raised. Then the match went out.

"Look here, Connie." He spoke softly. "I don't understand this."

"You don't understand what?"

"Just a moment. After you heard the shot, how long was it before you went up and looked through the window?"

"Oh, how can you expect me to be certain about times? I should think about two minutes. Maybe less."

"Yes. After you looked through the window and saw them, what did you do?"

"I didn't know what to do. I went back to the gate and stood there. Then I broke down and cried like a baby. I was still there when that policeman got here."

He nodded, inhaling smoke deeply. One sentence out of her recital, vivid in its artlessness, returned to him with powerful effect. *"He looked much, much more scared than he did when you and the policeman went in."* An innocent man, caught by circumstance? Yet Fred Barlow still did not understand, and said so.

"Don't you see," he pointed out, "that every word you've said tends to confirm your father's story?"

"Well—"

"He swears he didn't admit Morell to the bungalow. Confirmed. He swears that after picking up the revolver he just sat down in the chair and looked at it. Confirmed."

"Y-yes."

"Yes. Then why do you say you 'know' he shot Morell? Why are you so certain of it? If I remember rightly, as soon as you first spoke to him tonight you spoke as though you knew he did it. Why?"

No reply.

"Connie. Look at me. Is there anything you saw through that window that you haven't told me?"

"No!"

"You're quite sure?"

"Freddie Barlow, I'm not going to sit here and be cross-examined by you as though you didn't believe me. And I'm not afraid of you, either. You're not in court now. What I'm saying is true. If you don't a-appreciate what I'm trying to do, you can go and—and make love to Jane Tennant."

"God Almighty, what's Jane Tennant got to do with this?"

"I wonder."

"*What?*"

"Nothing."

"We were talking about your father. I can't understand why you're always throwing Jane Tennant in my teeth."

"She's absolutely scatty about you. But of course you hadn't seen that?"

"No. I repeat: we were talking about your father. Connie, this story of yours is true, isn't it?"

"Every word of it."

"Nothing left out?"

"Nothing left out, so help me."

The glowing end of the cigarette pulsed and darkened.

"Then Inspector Graham ought to know about it. It isn't complete confirmation, and it will probably be suspect as coming from you; but if it's true you stick to it and it will help. What I should like to learn—"

"Listen!" urged Constance, lifting her hand.

The partition walls of the bungalow were thin. From across the hall they were always conscious of a mutter of voices in the background. Now somebody thundered out with a ripe bit of profanity, followed by exclamations. They needed no acute wits to guess that the police had made a sufficiently startling discovery. His cigarette fell, and he trod it out.

Barlow hurried to the door. He did not trouble to conceal his presence, since nobody noticed him anyway. The door to the living-room was wide open, so that he could take in every detail of the scene.

Tony Morell's body lay in much the same place, some two or three feet out from the desk and parallel with its front. But, after being photographed from several angles, he had now been rolled over on his back. The telephone had been put back on the desk, its receiver in place. The overturned desk chair was now righted and pushed to one side.

Graham, Weems, and the two other officers were gathered absorbedly round the space on the floor between Morell's body and the desk.

On the sofa across the room sat Mr. Justice Ireton, smoking a cigar.

One of the men from Exeter spoke.

"I was born and bred in these parts," he declared. "I know 'em like the back of my hand. And I tell you straight, I never saw anything like it before."

Inspector Graham, the strawberry rash much in evidence, was argumentative.

"I still don't see it. What about the stuff? It's sand."

"Ah! But what kind of sand? That's what I'm asking you. What *kind* of sand?"

"All you've got to do," interposed Weems, with heavy portentousness, "is to walk along that there coast road, and sand blows at you. It gets on your coat and in your pockets and in the cuffs of your trousers—if you're wearing any. I mean, if you're wearing ordinary trousers and not a uniform. The chap got some himself. Look."

"Nuts, Albert," said the man from Exeter, who was evidently a keen student of the films. "See the amount of it, for one thing. There's enough to fill a two-ounce bottle in that little heap alone."

Inspector Graham stood back to study it, like a painter measuring perspective, and Fred Barlow had an uninterrupted view.

On the carpet, in a space hitherto hidden by the dead man's body, lay a small heap of sand. Before the body flattened it, it might have been vaguely pyramidal in shape; it had been not only flattened, but scattered. Grains and splashes of it were all over the carpet in that little space. A few grains clung to the damp-patched front of Morell's double-breasted grey suit. And this sand was clear to be seen because of its colour—a pale red.

"Red!" insisted their informant. "Every grain of sand in this district, I'll take my oath, is white. Bone-white."

Graham grunted.

"That's true," admitted PC Weems.

"So," pursued the other, "either this chap himself carried in a handful of sand from somewhere else, and poured it out on the floor. Or else the bloke who killed him poured it on the floor, and dropped him down on it."

Graham rounded on him.

"Don't talk soft," the Inspector said sternly. "And remember who's your superior officer."

"All right! I'm bound to tell you, that's all. And there's no sand in this room, because Tom and I have been over every nook and cranny of it."

"But why should anybody want to go pouring sand on the floor?"

Across the room, Mr. Justice Ireton took the cigar out of his mouth and blew a smoke ring. His expression seemed unguarded; he could not know anybody watched him from the hall; and Barlow could have sworn he was as puzzled as the officers.

"I ask you," demanded Graham. "Why should anybody want to go pouring sand on the floor?"

"Can't say—sir," grinned the tormentor. "That's your job. You have a pint at The Feathers and work it out. Tom and I want to get home. Anything else?"

The Inspector hesitated.

"No. Send those pictures over in the morning. Wait! What's the final fingerprint result?"

"Corpse's prints on telephone and receiver. OK. Few corpse's prints, smudged, on edge of desk and arm of desk chair. Otherwise, only the old gent's—" He stopped abruptly, hunching up his shoulders.

"That's all right," observed Mr. Justice Ireton. "I don't mind being referred to as the old gent. Pray continue."

"Thank you, sir. Only *his* prints, old ones, all over the place. His prints on the gun; grip, sides, and chamber. Yours too, Inspector. Nothing else, though there's smudges as though somebody touched it with gloves."

"Appleby," nodded Graham. "All right. You can go home. And don't try to be so ruddy funny next time."

Barlow waited until the unrepentant pair had gone, with

Weems escorting them. Then he went into the living-room. Graham regarded him without interest, and Mr. Justice Ireton with a sudden sharp snap of anger.

"I thought I instructed you," he said, "to take Constance home."

"She's not feeling up to it yet, I'm afraid. I came in to get her a brandy, if you don't mind."

After a slight hesitation, his host nodded curtly towards the sideboard. Barlow went to it, ran his eye along the row of bottles, and selected an excellent Armagnac. That should stiffen her back, right enough. While Barlow poured two fingers of brandy into a tumbler, Inspector Graham prowled moodily round the body. From the swivel-chair he picked up its rather grimy cushion, and slapped at it; and more grains of red sand ran down.

"Sand!" exploded Graham, flinging back the cushion. "Sand! Can you tell me anything about it, sir?"

"No," said Mr. Justice Ireton.

"There wasn't any of the stuff in the house, that you know of?"

"There was not."

Graham was dogged.

"You see what I'm getting at. Somebody brought the stuff in. Either Mr. Morell, or—somebody else. When was the last time you remember that there was no sand there? For instance, when was the last time you were in this room before you heard the shot?"

Mr. Justice Ireton sighed. "I have been waiting for you to ask that question, Inspector. I was sitting in this room until twenty minutes past eight, when I went out to the kitchen to prepare a meal. There was no sand here then."

"Twenty minutes past eight." Graham noted it down.

"Do you usually get your own dinner on Mrs. Drew's night out?"

"No. I detest fiddling with pots and pans. Ordinarily, as I think I told you, I spend Saturday in Town. I don't come down here until late, when I can dine on the train and get here in comfort about bedtime. But tonight, expecting a visitor—"

"So this room was empty for ten minutes, between eight-twenty and eight-thirty?"

"Pardon me. I can't say how long it was empty. I can only tell you Mr. Morell was here dead when I returned."

"Did you notice the sand then, sir?"

"Certainly not. Did *you*, until the body was rolled over?"

Graham shut his teeth hard.

"Well, was anything else different? Was there anything else different about the room, from the way you remember it when you went to the kitchen?"

Mr. Justice Ireton took two puffs at his cigar.

"Yes. The central lights were on."

"Lights?"

"The word should be familiar to you. Lights. That chandelier over your head. When I left the room, only the desk lamp was burning."

Fred Barlow, who had apparently been preoccupied in studying the brandy he had poured out, turned round from the sideboard.

"I think you ought to hear Miss Ireton's evidence, Inspector," he suggested.

"Miss Ireton? What evidence has she got?"

"Mr. Barlow," said the judge, with such a rush of blood to the head that his smooth cheeks were stained, "do me the favour of keeping out of this. My daughter has no concern with this affair."

"Admitted, sir. But she has something to tell which I think will help you."

"Are you under the impression that I *need* help, Mr. Barlow?"

(Danger! Look out! You've said the wrong thing!)

The hand which held the judge's cigar shook. Shifting the cigar to his left hand, he again took his spectacles out of his breast pocket and began to swing them. It had been a long, long evening. What Barlow feared was that they would now be treated to an exhibition of pure childish temper, which occurred seldom but which formed the other side of Horace Ireton's unemotional nature.

"I refuse to have my daughter mixed up in this," he said.

"Excuse *me*," interposed Graham heavily, "but maybe I'm the best judge of that. I've got to remind you that I'm in charge here."

"I refuse to have my daughter questioned."

"And I say that if Miss Ireton's got anything to tell me, it's her duty to come here and tell it."

"You insist on that?"

"Yes, sir, I do."

The judge's eyes opened wide.

"Take care, Inspector."

"I'll take care all right, sir! Mr. Barlow, will you…?"

What might have developed then, if there had not been an interruption, would not have done credit to anybody. It was a skidding of the wheel, a brief outlet for tempers, cut short by the entrance of PC Weems from the hall.

"Dr. Fell's here, Inspector," he reported. "The gentleman you 'phoned for."

Graham pulled himself up, bulging under his blue tunic. His face wore a faint mechanical smile which seemed to indicate that everything would be all right if only he had half a second to think.

"And there's a young lady with him," Weems continued, "the young lady who drove him over here. She'd like to come in too, sir, if you've got no objection. Her name's Tennant— Miss Jane Tennant."

CHAPTER X

THE MOMENTARY DANGER DRAINED AWAY AND WAS gone.

"Inspector," said Mr. Justice Ireton, "I beg your pardon. That was very foolish of me. You have, of course, a perfect right to question anyone whose evidence you think may be relevant. Pray forgive my lapse of manners."

"That's all right, sir!" Graham assured him, swelling with relief and heavily jovial. "I expect I spoke a bit short myself. No offence." His glance at Weems was ominous. "Tennant? Tennant? Who is she?"

"She's a friend of Miss Ireton's," Barlow answered for him. "Lives in Taunton."

Graham kept his eyes on Weems.

"Oh? What does she want? I mean, has she got any evidence to give us, or is she just here socially, like?"

"She didn't say, Inspector."

Graham crushed the unfortunate constable with a look, and turned to Barlow.

"Do you know her personally, sir?"

"Yes; quite well."

"Then do me a favour, will you? Go out and see her. Find out what she wants. If she's got anything to tell us, bring her in. If not—well, you know. Just be tactful, and send her away. We can't have people running about the house at a time like this. You, Bert, ask Dr. Fell to come in."

Carrying the brandy, Barlow hurried across to the bedroom. He found Constance standing by the rocking-chair as though she had just returned from listening at the door.

"How do you feel? Up to facing it?"

"Yes, if I've got to."

"Then drink this. No, don't sip it; gulp it down. The great Dr. Fell is here, to have a whack at things. It'll take a little while to haul him up and settle him down, which is all to the good. I've got to leave you for a moment, but I'll be back in time to stand by."

"Where are you going?"

"Back in a moment!"

He opened the catch of the middle window, and slipped out.

Weems, treading pontifically, was nearly to the gate. Barlow waited until the sound of voices had died away. A series of excruciating wheezes, and a thud, told him that Dr. Fell had wormed out of the car and set foot on the ground.

Fred stood on one side until Dr. Fell, in cape and shovel-hat, had followed Weems up the path. Then he opened the gate. A big two-seater Cadillac, engine throbbing, was drawn up on the far side of the road. Its headlamps shone out across the edge of earth, scrub grass, and sand. From the sea a great soft wind swept across the road. When he felt it stir his hair and deaden his eyelids, Fred Barlow thought: I'm damned tired.

"Hullo, Jane."

"Hullo, Fred."

These two had always been very bright and cheerful with each other. That seemed to have been the keynote of their acquaintance. Both were now very much subdued.

"The constable told me," observed Jane, "that 'Mr. Barlow would see me.' It's all right. I don't really want to go up there. Unless I can help Connie in any way?"

"You've heard about it, then?"

"Yes, the Inspector gave Dr. Fell the gist of it over the 'phone."

He leaned on the door of the car and put his head inside. Jane sat on the far side, behind the wheel, with a big expanse of red-leather cushion between them. Her face was turned sideways, partly lighted by the glow of the dashboard lamp. It was warm inside the bonnet of the car. He could feel the engine throb as he leaned his elbows on the door.

Tight little nerves, symbols of weariness, ached in the calves of his legs. End of assizes. Five difficult briefs. Four wins and a loss—Lypiatt.

'Taken hence to the place whence you came, and thence to the place of execution, there to be hanged by the neck until you are dead; and may God have mercy upon your soul.'

He flung away this thought. He was glad to see Jane Tennant. Not with the ordinary passive acceptance which that term usually implies; but with a warm and active rush of pleasure which ran through his whole mind.

She was a grand person. By gad, she was! Her very quietness was soothing. He noticed the slim hands on the steering-wheel, the tapering fingers and nails without varnish. He noticed the grey, wide-set eyes looking at him.

"How bad is it?" Her tone was guarded. "Dr. Fell thought the judge might be—involved. More than involved."

"Oh, it's not as bad as that. Do you mind if I climb in and sit down for a moment?"

Jane hesitated.

"Please do," she said.

He noted that hesitation. It damped his pleasure. She was always like this. It was not that she avoided him, or had ever been anything except perfectly friendly. Yet she always seemed to be moving away from him; to be putting a space between them, both figuratively and literally. If they were taking tea together (for instance), and there was room for two to sit on a sofa, she always moved across and sat in another chair. He reflected on this, thinking what a rotten judge of character Constance Ireton must be.

"There's plenty of room," she remarked. "There was almost room for Dr. Fell, and heaven knows that's recommendation enough." She laughed nervously, and checked herself. "I always say that these Cadillacs are spacious enough inside, but I can't get used to these American cars with the left-hand drive. They—"

He sat back on the red-leather cushions.

"Jane," he said, "can you help us?"

"Help you?"

"Tell us anything in the way of evidence."

She was silent for a long time. She had not even, he

reflected, turned off the engine. Its throbbing animated the feeling of loneliness and remoteness which had closed round this car. He had never been so conscious of Jane's physical presence.

"I want to be fair, Fred," she said at length. "I *did* know something about his history. That business—five years ago—"

"Yes." His head ached. "That's true, is it? If it's the case I read about, I can remember the details. It's true? It's the same Morell?"

"It couldn't be any other. And yet I can't understand it! Dr. Fell says, at least by what Mr. Graham told him, that Morell isn't the impecunious you-know-what. Graham says he's a well-to-do man with a flourishing business. It couldn't be a brother or something, could it?"

"No, it's the same man."

"But do you understand it?"

"Yes, I think I do." He stared at the dials on the dashboard. "It's Latin logic, that's all. Morell, or Morelli, thought he had a perfect right to capitalize his fascination powers over women. Not crookedness: logic. Then he got a jolt. Society caught him and made a fool of him in open court. So he made his resolve; he applied the same logic and the same hard work to building up another kind of business. It all hangs together. It's possible to follow every move he made."

"How well," said Jane, not without faint irony, "how well you judge people!"

He caught that irony, and it angered him.

"Thanks. Joking aside, though, he wasn't any better because he'd made good financially. Do you know, Jane, I hate him even after he's dead."

"Poor Fred."

"Why do you say 'Poor Fred'?"

"Just a way of speaking. Sympathizing with you, if you like. I didn't mean anything by it."

"Jane, what have I done to offend you?"

"You haven't done anything to offend me. May I have a cigarette?"

He fumbled in his pocket and produced the packet. She was sitting close against the other door, her arm along it and her breast rising and falling.

He handed her a cigarette, moved along towards her to light it, and struck a match. The light of the dashboard-lamps was on her face, and they looked each other straight in the eyes. He held the match level until it had burned half way down. Then he blew it out, and took the cigarette out of her mouth. He saw her eyes begin to close.

A clear voice said: "I do hope I'm not interrupting anything." And Constance Ireton appeared on the running-board.

There was a pause.

"He promised to come back," Constance went on, "and stand by me. I couldn't understand what was delaying him."

Fred Barlow did not look at Jane. He felt one complete seething mass of guilt, through every vein of him. Nor did Jane look at him. She shifted one foot to the clutch, and began revving the motor with the other; its roar beat out against emptiness, above the wash of the sea.

"I must get along home," said Jane, when she could make herself heard. "I'm a bad enough hostess as it is, leaving those people there. But—I heard about it, Connie. I'm terribly sorry about everything."

"I'm sure you are," agreed Constance. She waited a second or two. "You don't mind if I'm a little late in getting back to Taunton, dear? The police want to see me."

"No, of course not. Will you be all right?"

"Yes. I borrowed your Bentley."

"I know you did," said Jane, engaging bottom gear. "You'll find a spare petrol-tin under the back seat. Goodnight."

"Goodnight, dear. Fred, they want to see you in the house."

The villain of the piece crawled out of the car. They all said goodnight again, and the car moved away. Constance and Fred waited until the red tail-light had dwindled away down the road towards Horseshoe Bay; then he held open the gate. Not a word was spoken until they had nearly reached the bungalow.

"Well," said Constance, "aren't you going to explain yourself?"

(No, he was damned if he would!)

"Explain what?"

"You know what. I thought I could *depend* on you."

"You're well aware that you can depend on me, Connie."

"What were you two doing out there?"

He wanted to reply, "Nothing. You didn't give us a chance." Remembering what she had been through that night, he checked himself, and said:

"Nothing."

"You're going to her swimming-party tomorrow night, I suppose?"

"What swimming-party?"

"At the Esplanade Hotel. Dinner, and dancing, and then a late swim in that big indoor pool. Don't say she didn't invite you! She looks rather wonderful in a bathing-suit."

He stopped short.

In the living-room, through the gauze-net curtains on the windows, he could see Dr. Fell bending over Morell's body. PC Weems, kneeling beside it, was engaged in taking out the contents of the dead man's pockets. Graham watched him. So did Mr. Justice Ireton, who puffed at the stump of a cigar.

"Look in there," he said. "I'm not going to any swimming-party. Neither are you. Neither, Lord help us, is your old man. There's the reason why. For the love of Mike stop talking about Jane Tennant, and—" He drew in his breath. "Besides, what difference does it make? You're not interested in me."

"No. Not like that. But I'm used to having you about, Fred. I'm used to depending on you. I can't give that up. I *can't*!—especially now." Her voice grew hysterical. "It's been pretty awful, you know. You won't desert me, will you?"

"All right."

"Promise?"

"Promise. Now in you go, and don't show yourself till they call you."

Yet a vision of Jane Tennant's face flicked through his mind as he sent Constance into the hall, and himself entered the living-room by the window. He caught Inspector Graham at the end of a patient summary.

"And that, Doctor, is every bit of evidence we've got to date. Would you like to give any opinion—offhand?"

Dr. Fell's cape and shovel-hat lay on the sofa beside Mr. Justice Ireton. Dr. Fell himself turned slowly round on his stick, like a liner easing into port, and surveyed each part of the room in turn. His expression was vague and almost half-witted. The ribbon on his eyeglasses drooped. Yet Barlow, who had heard him testify many times in court, was not deceived.

"What bothers me most, sir, is the red sand," Graham confessed.

"Oh, ah! Why?"

"*Why?*" demanded the Inspector. "What's it doing there? What's the meaning of it? Where did it come from? I'd lay you a bob you can't think of any reasonable explanation for keeping an ounce or so of red sand in anybody's house."

"You would lose your bob," said Dr. Fell. "What about an hour-glass?"

There was silence.

Mr. Justice Ireton had closed weary eyelids.

"Like the man in the *Punch* story," he said snappily, "I find it much simpler to carry a watch. There are no hour-glasses here."

"Are you sure?" asked Dr. Fell. "Many housewives use 'em—they're minute-glasses, really—for boiling eggs. They usually contain reddish sand; first because it's very fine-grained, and second because it's easy to see. What about your housekeeper here?"

Inspector Graham whistled.

"That might be it! Come to think of it, I've seen those things, too. You think that's it?"

"I have not the remotest idea," admitted Dr. Fell. "I only said you would lose your bob if you wagered nobody could explain it." He mused. "Besides, that's paler sand than you see in most glasses. To my scatter-brain it vaguely suggests a name. Lake Something. Lake—No, it's gone." His big face smoothed itself out. "But if you asked me what bothered me the most, Inspector, I should say the telephone."

"The telephone? What about it?"

While Mr. Justice Ireton watched him, Dr. Fell went across and blinked at it. It was some time before he answered.

"You observe that there's a piece knocked off the edge of the mouthpiece, and a crack along the side as well. Hey?"

"It fell off on the floor."

"Yes. Granted. And this is not a very thick carpet." He tested it with his foot. "Still, I have my doubts. I myself have sometimes knocked the telephone off my own desk. In fact, while gesturing during moments of eloquence, I have once or twice sent the blighter flying. But I never remotely managed to do the damage that seems to have been done to this one."

"All the same, it *was* done."

"Yes: it was done. Let us see."

Stepping over Morell's body, he propped his stick against the desk, picked up the telephone, and began clumsily to unscrew the mouthpiece. It came away after some difficulty with the threads.

Dr. Fell held it up to the light, peered through the perforations of the inside, and sniffed at it. He frowned. But when he picked up the 'phone itself, where the delicate sounding-drum was now exposed by the removal of the mouthpiece, he uttered an exclamation.

"Cracked," he pointed out. "This microphone part— cracked. That, surely, suggests something to us. No wonder the later sounds heard by the girl at the exchange were confused and meaningless."

"I knew it was out of kilter," Graham admitted. "When I

tried to 'phone you at the hotel I had such trouble with this one that I finally used the extension in the kitchen. But how does it help us even if the telephone *is* smashed?"

Dr. Fell was not listening. He set down the telephone after an unsuccessful attempt to screw the mouthpiece back in again. He seemed even more startled and worried.

"No, no, no, no!" he observed, as though sceptically, to nobody in particular. "No, no, no, no!"

Inspector Graham exchanged an exasperated glance with Mr. Justice Ireton. The latter consulted his watch.

"The hour," he said, "is late."

"It is, sir," agreed Graham. "And we haven't even had Miss Ireton in yet. Got the stuff out of Morell's pockets, Bert?"

"All here, Inspector," replied PC Weems, who had been arranging articles in a neat line on the carpet.

"Well?"

"First, these three packets of banknotes…"

"Yes, yes, we've seen 'em! Well?"

"Notecase with four-pound-ten in it, and some business cards. Nine and elevenpence in silver and coppers. Bunch of keys on ring. Address book. Pencil and fountain-pen. Pocket comb. Packet of Toni-Sweet Peppermint Chewing-Gum, one or two sticks gone. That's the lot."

Dr. Fell, though he listened, did not appear interested. He picked up the cushion of the swivel desk chair, and blinked at it. While Weems droned on, he wandered over to the chess table, where he picked up the revolver. Holding it sideways to the light, so that he could see the tiny cross cut into the steel under the magazine-chamber, he glanced at Mr. Justice Ireton.

Not until he had put down the gun again did the judge speak.

"You're still a bad chess player," he said.

"So? Is my dial as expressive as all that?"

"Yes."

"What does it tell you?"

"That you're still a bad chess player."

"Anything else?"

Mr. Justice Ireton reflected, his lips pursed. "Yes, I think so. My dear Fell, I never realized until this minute how much you dislike me."

"*I?* Dislike you?"

Mr. Justice Ireton made a gesture of impatience. "Oh, not me personally, perhaps!"

"Then may I venture to inquire what in blazes you did mean?"

"I mean my principles. They irk your sentimental soul. I would not insult your intelligence by referring to feelings, friendly or unfriendly. There is hardly anything in this world of less value than relationships based on mere feeling."

Dr. Fell stared at him.

"You really believe that?"

"I am not in the habit of saying things I don't mean."

"H'mf, well. Descending to the personal—"

"Oh, yes; I understand. I have a daughter. I am fond of her, being only human. But nature has seen to that. I can't help myself, any more than I can help having two arms and legs. Even in that feeling"—his little eyes opened—"even in that feeling, there are limits. You follow me?"

Dr. Fell sighed. "Yes," he said. "I thought you were stating a creed. Now I see we're only playing chess."

Mr. Justice Ireton did not bother to reply.

The spacious room, with its bilious blue-flowered wallpaper, was silent except for the scratching of Graham's pen as he docketed the articles in Morell's pockets.

Dr. Fell absentmindedly pulled open the drawer of the chess table. Finding the chess pieces in their wooden box with the sliding lid, he began with ferocious absentmindedness to toy with them. He set out a king, a bishop, a knight. He picked up a pawn, and turned it over in his hand. He tossed it into the air and caught it with a flat smack against his palm. He tossed it again. He tossed it a third time. Suddenly he dropped it; and, as though struck by a memory, made a huge inhalation of breath.

"O Lord!" he breathed. "O Bacchus! O my ancient hat!"

Inspector Graham turned round from writing at the desk.

"Get Miss Ireton, Bert," he said.

Once before the tribunal, Constance made an admirable witness. Her father kept his eyes on the floor, as though not to upset her, but his ears seemed to be straining for every word.

She told how she had seen Morell enter by the French window at twenty-five minutes past eight. She told how the central lights had been turned on immediately afterwards. She told how she had been sitting down on the bank, facing the sea, when she heard the shot. She told how she had gone up to the bungalow afterwards, and peered briefly through the window.

Then they came to the part in which she had been coached in lies by Barlow, and Barlow held his breath.

"I see, miss," observed Inspector Graham, very suspicious yet clearly impressed. "There's one thing I'm not clear about, though. Why did you come here tonight?"

"To see Daddy."

"You didn't know Mr. Morell was coming here to see him?"

Her eyes widened. "Oh, no! You see, Tony had gone to London that morning. I didn't expect him back in Taunton until late that night, if he came back at all."

"But what I'm getting at," frowned Graham, "is this. You borrowed this car. It broke down. You walked to the bungalow here, and saw Mr. Morell coming along the road. Why was it you didn't call out to him, or show yourself?" Constance lowered her eyes modestly.

"I—well, as soon as I saw him, I guessed what he must be there for. He and Daddy were meeting to talk about *me*. Probably that wedding-present Daddy said was so generous of Tony. I didn't want to be there, embarrassing them and me too. So I thought I'd just wait a while, and then go in casually as though I knew nothing about it."

Mr. Justice Ireton kept his eyes on the floor. Fred Barlow's mind was warm with professional satisfaction. And Inspector Graham nodded.

"Yes, miss," he said, after an inner struggle, "that does seem reasonable enough, I'm bound to admit."

Twenty minutes later it was all over. The local police surgeon, a harassed GP who attended to this job in addition to his ordinary practice, arrived in a flurry as Constance finished. He explained his lateness as due to a difficult confinement. He pointed out that Morell had died as the result of a wound from a small-calibre bullet, which penetrated the brain and killed him instantly. After promising to extract the bullet first thing in the morning, Dr. Early waved his hat at everybody and hurried away.

Morell's body was removed in a basket. Fred Barlow drove Constance to Taunton. Mr. Justice Ireton said that he had no objection whatever to spending the night here; tonight, or any other night. By half past eleven, when all the West Country was sealed up in sleep, Dr. Fell and Inspector Graham had themselves returned to Tawnish.

As the Inspector deposited Dr. Fell on the steps of the Esplanade Hotel, the latter spoke for perhaps the first time in an hour.

"One final thing," he said, plucking at Graham's arm. "You made a thorough search of that living-room?"

"We did that, sir!"

"Every chink and cranny of it?"

"Every chink and cranny of it."

"Without," insisted Dr. Fell, "finding anything whatever except what we know?"

"That's right, Doctor. But," Graham added significantly, "I'll ring you up in the morning, if you don't mind. I'd like to have a little chat with you. OK?"

Dr. Fell assented. Yet he was not satisfied. As he climbed the steps of the hotel, whose lamps were out and whose ornate garishness was now veiled by starlight, he struck the ferrule of his stick sharply on the stones. Several times he shook his head with obstinate determination.

"No, no, no, no!" he kept on muttering, as once before that night. "No, no, no, no!"

CHAPTER XI

THAT WAS THE NIGHT OF SATURDAY, APRIL twenty-eighth. On Sunday morning it was past noon before Inspector Graham could reach Dr. Gideon Fell.

For many persons it had been a night touched with dreams.

Inspector Graham read through his notes, smoked a last pipe, and slept soundly afterwards.

Herman Appleby, the solicitor—who spent the night at a place nobody expected—went to bed commendably early, after winding up his watch and putting his false teeth in a glass of water.

Fred Barlow dreamed of Jane Tennant, and of the idea Connie Ireton had put into his head. His subconscious mind moved in the direction for which it had always been intended from the first.

In the big white house outside Taunton, Jane Tennant herself moved in restless sleep, turning from side to side.

Constance Ireton slept only after getting up to take two Luminal pills from the medicine cabinet in the bathroom.

On her way back she paused outside Jane's door. She listened to the muttering inside. She opened the door. She sat down softly on a chair beside the bed, and listened again. Afterwards she slipped away to her own room, and drowsed off among many fancies.

Some distance away, in a private sanatorium, a girl named Cynthia Lee lay and stared with wide-open eyes at the ceiling.

Mr. Justice Ireton, in black silk pyjamas, sat up in bed reading Francis Bacon. The jewelled sentences pleased him. When he saw that he had read for the scheduled quarter of an hour, he turned out his light, slept, and did not dream at all.

Last of all to turn out his light was Dr. Fell. As the clock went on chiming through the night he sat behind the table in his hotel bedroom, smoking a black pipe which he frequently replenished with tobacco tasting like the steel-wool that is used to clean kitchen sinks. The room was poisonous with smoke, and dawn had begun to come up over the sea when he opened his windows before turning in.

So it was well past noon when the shrilling of the telephone-bell beside his bed roused him.

He stretched out a hand for it.

"*Good* morning, sir," said Inspector Graham's voice, with austerity. "I rang before, but they said you'd given orders never to disturb you before noon."

"You are now going to tell me," wheezed Dr. Fell, getting the morning cough out of his throat, "what Napoleon said. 'Six hours for the man, seven for the woman, and eight for the fool.' Blast Napoleon. I must have SLEEP."

Inspector Graham did not refer to Napoleon.

"The bullet that killed Mr. Morell," he reported, "was

fired from that revolver. Captain Ackley says there's no doubt about that."

"Had you ever any doubt of it?"

"No; but you know how these things are. Next, we've traced Mr. Morell's movements. The eight o'clock train from London last night was seven minutes late. At eight-ten or a little later, Morell asked to be put right for the coast road. The witness remembers particularly because he was peeling the wrapper off a stick of chewing-gum, and wolfing at it like he wanted to eat it. That gives him something under fifteen minutes, between then and eight-twenty-five, to walk the rest of the distance—which is about right."

"Well?"

"We've got in touch with Mr. Morell's only relative in this country. A brother, Luigi Morelli. Head-waiter at the Isis Hotel in London."

"How did you hear about him?"

"From Mr. Appleby. Last night. Now, when can I come and see you for a bit of gabfest about this business?"

"Come and have lunch with me here," said Dr. Fell, "in about an hour."

Graham sounded respectful though puzzled. "Very much obliged to you, sir. But you haven't had breakfast, have you?"

"I shall have breakfast now," explained Dr. Fell simply, "and lunch in about an hour. Surely the problem is easy of solution. Until then!"

He rang off, found and adjusted his eyeglasses, and settled back against a mountain of pillows to ponder. Presently he took up the 'phone again. After a long and somewhat acrimonious conversation with the exchange, he was put through to Fred Barlow's cottage at Horseshoe Bay.

Barlow, though he sounded surprised, readily accepted the doctor's invitation to lunch in about an hour.

"I'd thought of going over to Taunton," he said. "But if it's something important to do with this—"

"Very important," rumbled Dr. Fell.

"Right-o. Thanks very much."

It was a fine morning, as warm as the middle of May. False warmth. In the pleasant sitting-room of his cottage, Fred Barlow tapped his fingers on the telephone and pondered in his turn.

He should have had a good night's sleep, but he did not look rested. He was fidgety and inclined to prowl. Mr. Justice Ireton would have deprecated this.

Sunlight streamed warm through the windows on old books, a pair of oars whose grips he was mending, and a general comfortable untidiness. He changed his tie, and read slowly through the *Sunday Times* to allow himself leeway. Then he got out his car, which he had retrieved from the roadside—it reminded him of the encounter there, and the shapeless figure on the ground—and he drove slowly to Tawnish without stopping at the judge's bungalow.

The Esplanade itself was deserted. The entrance-lounge of the Esplanade Hotel was large, ghostly, and empty except for two persons.

One was Herman Appleby, burnished for Sunday morning, sitting in an easychair and glancing through a newspaper.

The other was Jane Tennant.

He saw Jane first, and took a step towards her. But the

solicitor anticipated him by rising in leisurely fashion, dusting the newspaper out of his hands, and approaching with a cordial smile.

"Mr. Barlow, isn't it?"

"Yes. Mr. Appleby? What are you doing here?"

"It hardly seemed worth while driving all the way back to London last night. If I can find a barber open on Sunday morning"—Appleby rubbed his cheek, by way of illustration—"I shall feel happy again. Beautiful morning for a walk, isn't it?"

"Fine, I suggest—"

"You don't happen to know," inquired Appleby, lowering his voice and drawing his eyebrows together, "whether Mr. Justice Ireton spent last night at his bungalow? Or possibly at some more congenial place?"

"He's still there, as far as I know. But he's usually pretty touchy at this time of day."

"Well! We all are, sometimes," said Appleby. "Thank you."

He went back to pick up his bowler hat from beside the chair. He dusted it off, lifted it at Fred by way of farewell, and pushed out through the revolving doors. After a hesitation, Fred walked across to Jane. She followed the same formula.

"What," she asked, "are *you* doing here?"

"Dr. Fell invited me to lunch. And you?"

"Dr. Fell invited me too—"

They both stopped.

Fred Barlow had never been more conscious that he was not looking his best. He was not unshaven, but he felt unshaven. On the other hand, he had never before noticed how genuinely and even brilliantly good-looking Jane Tennant was. She wore blue, with white at the neck and wrists.

"I told him I had a house full of guests, and couldn't possibly come." She laughed a little. "But he simply wouldn't take no for an answer. Not that most of that casual crowd ever notice whether I'm in the house or not. Besides, I had an excuse."

"Excuse?"

"To come here. I'm giving a swimming-party here tonight. At the Esplanade. I said I had to see the manager." She hesitated. "As a matter of fact, I wanted to call it off, because of Connie. But the others are clamouring for it, and I don't see how I can."

"How is Connie?"

"Feeling beastly. She started to pack her bags to go back to London. But I told her there would be nobody at her father's house there; and here at least she'd be among friends who would take care of her. I think I managed to persuade her."

"That dress becomes you, Jane."

"It's the old story. All you've got to do is put on blue, and *any* man thinks you look well."

"No, I mean it! It—"

"Thank you, sir. This party tonight is just a little affair. Very informal. Dinner, dancing, and drinks beside the pool. I don't suppose you'd care to come along, would you? Or do you—indulge?"

He detested dancing, but he was a very fine swimmer.

"I'd like to very much," he said, "if you don't mind whether I'm a little late."

"Not a bit! Any time at all. You can bring your own bathing-suit, or get one here. It's—it's mostly that rather arty crowd you're not fond of; but if it wouldn't bore you—?"

"Good God! Bore me!" he said suddenly, and then checked himself.

"That's settled then. Shall we go upstairs? Dr. Fell said to go upstairs. I know the number of his room."

A vision of Constance Ireton's face came into his mind as he followed Jane to the lift.

"I didn't know," he suggested, trying to find a relief for this by changing the subject, "you were so well acquainted with Dr. Fell."

"Oh, we're old friends."

She pressed the bell for the lift, quickly. "I didn't know you were a friend of his."

"I'm not. I've met him once or twice before last night, and heard him testify in court." New doubts, sharp new suspicions, wormed into Fred Barlow's mind. "He's the decentest bloke in the world, but academically he's a terror. He can split a hair sixteen ways and still have something left over. If he likes you he can't do enough for you. Of course you'd know that. But I was just wondering what he's got up his sleeve *now*."

What Dr. Fell had up his sleeve did not immediately become apparent.

He welcomed them in his room, one vast substantial beam like the Ghost of Christmas Present, wearing a shiny black alpaca suit and a string tie. On a little balcony outside sun-filled windows overlooking the promenade, a lunch table was set with places for four.

"We eat," explained Dr. Fell, "on the balcony. I am very

fond of eating on balconies; or, in fact, anywhere else. But it is a particular source of satisfaction—as Mr. Justice Ireton would say—to sit godlike above the passing throng; reflecting (should the evil impulse occur) what emotions could be aroused below by the dexterous use of bread-pellets or a soda-water syphon. You know this gentleman, I think?"

Behind him Fred Barlow was startled to see the ominous-looking figure of Inspector Graham.

"I've met Mr. Barlow," said Graham, who as a concession to hospitality had removed his uniform-cap, and was now revealed as pinkly bald. "Haven't had the pleasure of meeting the young lady."

"Inspector Graham, Miss Tennant. Shall we go and get it?"

Definitely, the doctor was up to something.

Throughout the meal Graham's manner was pleasant but not encouraging. He seemed to have something on his mind, and to wish there were no other guests except himself. Also, he was unfortunately placed with his back to the wrought-iron railing of the balcony, so that the sun struck his bald head.

That lunch, under his disturbing eye, should have been a failure. True, they ate good food. They drank good claret, and rather a lot of it, though Graham held out for bitter. But that it was not a failure was due to Dr. Fell, who told stories until even Graham suddenly sat back and roared.

After each story he would raise his eyebrows cherubically, as though he wondered that they should see anything funny in it, and tell another.

All the same, even in the midst of this, something nagged at the back of Fred Barlow's mind. He felt that he could really let go and enjoy himself *if—*

The black spot again? Or Jane Tennant's presence? Jane, he noticed, was preoccupied. Beyond them, the sea lay slate-grey shading to smoky purple; the houses along the front were gabled and painted like those in a Walt Disney film.

Coffee and brandy arrived. Three cigars and a box of cigarettes were laid on the table. Leaning across to light Jane's cigarette, Fred remembered last night. And Dr. Fell approached the subject to be discussed with all the gradual-ness and delicacy of a load of bricks falling through a skylight.

"This meeting," he announced, rapping on the table, "will come to order. Minutes read and approved. Your chairman suggests that Inspector Graham open the proceedings by telling us why he thinks Mr. Justice Ireton is, or is not, guilty of murder."

CHAPTER XII

Inspector Graham's expression said, "I knew it!" He threw his napkin on the table. But Dr. Fell held up an admonitory hand.

"One moment!" he insisted, puffing out his cheeks. "I put the matter thus bluntly because here we have a different kind of problem from the usual one. The vital question, to us, is different. The vital question is not: Who might have committed this murder? The vital question is: *Did Mr. Justice Ireton commit it?*

"As for possible or potential murderers, they are all over the place. I can think of two or three offhand. I might even construct a case against them. But all this is swept away by a narrower, more vexing and tantalizing personal question: Did he, or didn't he?

"It is vexing from its very simplicity. Did this much-feared gentleman himself go off the rails, as he thought he never could? Or is he just the victim of that 'circumstantial evidence' which he himself thinks can't close round an innocent man? There you have it."

Dr. Fell lit his cigar.

"Consequently," he went on, "I thought it might be instructive if we had a discussion. With, say, Mr. Barlow acting as counsel for the defence—"

Barlow interrupted.

"I can't do that," he said sharply. "And I wouldn't if I could. Is it suggested that the judge needs defending? Or that his position is, or ever could be, questionable? Nonsense!"

"H'mf. Well. Ask Inspector Graham what *he* thinks."

Graham's strawberry rash was conspicuous. He spoke with persuasiveness, and some dignity.

"And *I* say, sir, that I can't discuss it either. In public, I mean. You ought to see that. I came here believing—"

"That you and I would have a private pow-wow? Hey?"

"If you like. I'm sure Mr. Barlow understands my position." Graham smiled. "And I'm sure the young lady does too," he added, with powerful gallantry. "I've got my duty to do. I can't go about airing my opinions, even if I had any."

Dr. Fell sighed.

"Quite," he said. "I apologize. Then perhaps you won't mind if *I* discuss it?"

Graham's air was quiet and watchful, with a lurking expectancy in it.

"I can't very well prevent that, can I?"

The thought which flashed through Fred Barlow's mind was: I underestimated Graham. He thinks the old man's guilty. And that's a nasty bump to begin with.

"In arguing the case," pursued Dr. Fell, "we have got to go only by the admissible, legal evidence. Motive is no good to us. No good at all. You can say, if you like: suppose Horace

Ireton didn't know Morell was the wealthy owner of an honest business, and thought he was only a penniless blackmailer? Suppose he killed Morell to prevent this marriage?

"You can suppose that, but it will get you nowhere. You can't prove he didn't know that. You can't prove a man *didn't* know a thing, if he chooses to swear he did. If I announce that I know Columbus discovered America in 1492, and I have never before been questioned on the subject, you can't prove I was ignorant of the fact until yesterday. You may infer it, from my conversation. But you can't prove it.

"So let's look at the concrete facts about this murder, by which we may be able to prove something. What are those facts? On the night of April twenty-eighth, at half past eight in the evening, Anthony Morell was shot in the living-room of Mr. Justice Ireton's bungalow. The weapon employed was an Ives-Grant ·32 revolver—"

Fred Barlow interposed.

"Is that established, by the way?" he asked swiftly.

Inspector Graham hesitated. "Yes, sir. I'm not giving much away if I say it *is* established."

"An Ives-Grant ·32 revolver," continued Dr. Fell, "whose only distinguishing mark is a small cross cut into the steel under the magazine-chamber."

This was the point at which Jane Tennant upset her coffee.

It was a small cup, rocky on its saucer. We have all done the same thing with an incautious movement of the hand. And little coffee remained in it, so that there was no mess. Jane did not comment on it, and nobody else affected to notice. But Fred, now abnormally sensitive to atmosphere, felt from her an emotional wave he could not define.

She regarded Dr. Fell with grey, steady, thoughtful eyes. Her cheeks were faintly stained with colour. Dr. Fell did not look back at her.

"So that the gun may be difficult to trace. Very difficult to trace." He paused, wheezing. "Next, where were the various people concerned when this occurred? Mr. Justice Ireton was in the kitchen. Morell was in the living-room, at the telephone. Constance Ireton was down on the beach, under the slope of the bank, with her back to the bungalow. Mr. Barlow—"

Again he paused, this time abruptly, and ran a hand through his big grey-streaked mop of hair.

"One moment! Where *was* Mr. Barlow?" He looked at Fred. "The question, sir, has no sinister implication. It is simply that I have never heard."

"That's right," Inspector Graham agreed suddenly; and after another inner struggle he pursued the matter. "It does seem a pity to spoil a good dinner like this talking business. But it reminds me. Mr. Barlow, Bert Weems tells me that when he was going out to the judge's place on his bike last night he ran into you."

"That's right."

"He says your car was pulled up on the wrong side of the road, just about opposite the entrance to Lovers' Lane. He says you stopped him, and started to tell him something about 'a tramp,' or 'Dr. Fellows.' I intended to ask you last night, but it slipped my mind. What was it all about?"

"It was Black Jeff," replied Barlow. "He's back again."

Graham uttered an "Oh, ah!" of enlightenment, but Dr. Fell was merely bewildered.

"Black Jeff?" the doctor repeated. "Who or what is Black Jeff?"

Graham explained. "He's a bit of a thorn in our side. A tramp; or a vagrant, if you want to make the distinction. Always comes popping up here after long absences."

"Black Jeff. A n—o?"

"No; it's his hair and whiskers, which are pretty striking. I've seen men get drunk," said Graham, shaking his head reflectively, "but I never saw six men get as drunk, in a quiet way, as Jeff does. Where he gets the money for it nobody knows. We don't even know who serves him, because most publicans wouldn't. The trouble is that when he gets to saturation-point he just flops down and sleeps, wherever he happens to be in the street. He's harmless, and we don't like to run him in, but—golly!"

Fred's voice was grim. He saw again the black road, the distant-spaced street-lamps, the huddled figure.

"Well," Fred said, "he very nearly went to his eternal sleep last night."

"Oh?"

"Yes. I was driving into Tawnish to get some cigarettes. I was nearly to Lovers' Lane—" He turned to Dr. Fell. "That's a little side lane that joins the main road, at right angles, about three hundred yards away from the judge's cottage in the direction of Tawnish. An estate agent company once tried to 'develop' the building sites it leads to. There's a telephone-box and a couple of model houses up there; but the scheme fell through. I don't know whether you've noticed the road?"

"No," said Dr. Fell. "But go on."

"I was almost to Lovers' Lane when I saw Jeff lying almost

slap in the middle of the main road. As a matter of fact, when I first saw him I thought he'd been hit and run over. I stopped the car and got out. It was Jeff all right. Drunk as Davy's sow; but I couldn't tell whether he'd been hurt. I dragged him across to the opposite side of the road—towards the sea— and put him down on the sand.

"Just then Dr. Fellows's car came past and nearly walloped both of us. I told the doctor about it, but he only said, 'Rubbish; roll him down the bank: the tide'll sober him up,' and went on. Jeff didn't *seem* to be hurt, I admit; but I went to my car and got an electric torch to make sure. When I got back to the place I thought I'd left him, he was gone."

Both the Inspector and Dr. Fell blinked at him out of the smoke of their cigars.

"Gone?" repeated the former.

"Believe it or not, gone."

"But where?"

"I can't tell you. I still haven't got the remotest idea. At first I thought I must have mistaken the place where I left him. I walked all along there. Finally I backed my car, and pulled it over to the other side of the road so that the headlights could shine all along there. That's why the car was on the wrong side. But I didn't find him. Black whiskers and funny clothes and bandana handkerchief and all—he was just gone."

The Inspector grunted.

"Probably came to life when you moved him. Then got up and staggered away. Drunks do that."

"Yes, that's what I thought." Suddenly Fred Barlow found himself inwardly cold, so cold that it was difficult to control his muscles or his voice. He must not show this. He tightened every nerve in his body so that he should not show it.

"And yet," he added, "I still don't know whether he was hurt."

"Shouldn't trouble, if I were you," the Inspector said callously. "Jeff's the least of *my* worries. We can probably find him asleep in one of those model houses, if we should ever happen to want him."

"Yes. I hope so."

The shadow passed. Fred breathed again.

"Which," observed Dr. Fell, who had been obscurely musing while he sucked at his cigar like a peppermint-stick, "which disposes of another character. Where were the others? Mr. Herman Appleby was presumably driving round and round country lanes, having lost his way—"

"Ah," said Graham.

"And Miss Tennant was on her way to see me here—"

Jane regarded him dispassionately. "I hope you don't think I'm mixed up in the murder?"

Dr. Fell merely chuckled and shook his head. It was Graham who answered her.

"Hardly, miss. Still, you might be able to help. I think it was you who came along to the bungalow last night, with Dr. Fell, and asked if you could come in?"

"Yes, that's right."

"Had you anything you wanted to tell me?"

"No, I'm afraid not."

"You knew Mr. Morell, though? After all, you invited him to your house-party."

"Not exactly. I invited Connie Ireton and her boy-friend.

That's how things are done nowadays. I hadn't even heard his name until he got there."

"And you don't know anything more about Mr. Morell?"

Jane drew deeply at her cigarette, expelled smoke, and balanced the cigarette on the edge of the saucer.

"I know," she replied, "no more than Dr. Fell knows."

For some reason obscure to Fred Barlow, Dr. Fell was chuckling and rubbing his hands together with delight.

"Good girl!" he said. "Good girl!"

"Thank you," said Jane, and added under her breath: "Damn you."

"Now then," said Graham, almost on the edge of losing his temper, "what's all this? What's going on here? All I can say is that *I'd* like to know what Dr. Fell knows. You've got a reputation for being on the exasperating side, sir. And I don't mind telling you I can see how it works—now. You started out by saying you were going to discuss evidence. All you've done is drag in a lot of unimportant stuff that's got nothing to do with the case. What is this evidence you wanted to discuss?"

Dr. Fell's tone changed.

"Very well," he said sharply. "I can tell you short and sweet. The telephone."

There was a silence.

"The telephone in the living-room at the bungalow, you mean?"

"Yes. That curious instrument with a bad chip knocked out of the mouthpiece, and the sounding-drum broken inside. Mark that. Inside."

Graham's shrewd eyes studied him.

"I've been thinking about that, sir. That inside bit is

delicate, right enough. But I can't see how it could have been broken when the telephone fell on the floor. It was too much protected."

"It couldn't have been," said Dr. Fell. "It wasn't. Then how *was* it broken?" He took a reflective puff at his cigar. "You may or may not remember that when I unscrewed the mouthpiece of that 'phone I gave it a sniff?"

"Yes. I remember."

"Powder-grains," said Dr. Fell. "A distinct smell along the edge."

"I see. You think the inside bit was cracked by the noise of the shot?"

"That, and the pressure of gases expelled when a pistol is fired. You remember, our invaluable Weems quotes the girl at the exchange as saying that the noise nearly broke her eardrums."

Graham contemplated as though with half-growing comprehension. He opened his mouth to speak; but, after glancing at Jane and Fred, he checked himself. He raised his cigar, which had long ago gone out, as though he were going to cast a spell with it.

"That," pursued Dr. Fell, "that, I might meekly suggest, is a part of the truth. The inference which follows is obvious and will not escape you."

"I'm afraid it escapes me," said Jane. "The firing of a bullet can do that, I suppose?"

"Oh, yes. It can. It did."

The sun was lower now, nor did the balcony feel quite so pleasant as at the beginning of lunch. False warmth had begun to drain from the day, as it was draining from the case.

Yet a sprinkling of determined Sunday pleasure-seekers straggled along the promenade. Children and dogs shot among them like skittle-balls, and with much the same effect. Small cars glistened, each a family pride. A beach photographer snapped pictures and hoped for the best. A lorry was parked near some steps leading down to the sands, where three men were filling sandbags. This last sight had not, in those days, the grim and ugly significance it has acquired since; and at least three of the watchers on the balcony regarded it without curiosity.

Dr. Fell spoke after a long silence.

"That part of it is clear," he said. "The rest is obscure. Or shall we say mixed? A patch of light, a patch of darkness." He turned his head round sombrely. "Tell me, Miss Tennant. You know Constance Ireton fairly well?"

"Yes, I think so."

"Should you call her a particularly truthful person?"

Danger! Fred Barlow sat up straight.

Jane hesitated, glancing sideways at him before she looked back to Dr. Fell.

"I don't quite see how I can answer that," Jane said. "We're none of us 'particularly' truthful, if it comes to that. She's certainly as truthful as most people, anyway."

"I mean: she is not a romantic liar? She wouldn't lie for the sheer pleasure of it?"

"Oh, no!"

"This is getting interesting," said Inspector Graham, hitching his chair round. "Does that mean you're not satisfied with the young lady's story, sir?"

Again Dr. Fell was silent.

"H'mf," he growled. "Well—! It *sounds* right. It's so cir-cumstantial. It's convincing, particularly that detail about the lights going up. But—look here, Miss Tennant. I'll put at least one point up to you. Now, imagine that you're Constance Ireton."

"Yes."

"Imagine that Horace Ireton is your father, and that the man who was in love with her is in love with you."

At this point Jane turned round and tossed the stump of her cigarette over the balustrade. When she turned back, hers was a face of patient attention.

"Yes?"

"Very well. You borrow a car, thinking your lover has gone to London, and drive over to see your father. The car breaks down. You do the rest of a short distance on foot. When you are nearly to the bungalow you see Morell, on his way there. It occurs to you that these two are meeting to discuss *you*, and so you decide tactfully to keep out of the way for a little while. So far, so good!"

He put down the cigar and interlaced his fingers.

"But consider the next part of it. You go to the beach, sit down comfortably, and wait. Five minutes later you hear an unexpected noise. You can't see the source of this noise. The tide is high and thundering. The noise must be at least twenty or thirty yards away behind you. Do you immediately think (*a*) that's a revolver shot; (*b*) it came from the bungalow; and (*c*) it means trouble for me? Do you? Would you? And so hurry up to see?"

Dr. Fell paused.

"I mention the point because that's what she said she did.

Also, it was damp and had been raining. Constance Ireton wore a white frock. But I noticed no sign of sand or damp on the—harrumph—area which would be employed in sitting down."

Jane laughed. It was a brief laugh, more at his elephantine delicacy than because she saw anything funny in the matter. She grew grave.

"I don't see anything wrong," she said sharply.

"No?"

"No! Connie might have done just that, if she thought Morell was trying to... I *mean*—!"

It was a bad slip. Too late she tried desperately to recall or blot out the words. While a bursting silence held the table, Inspector Graham's eye was on her.

"Go on, miss," he requested without emotion. "You were going to say, 'If she thought Morell was trying to get money out of her father.' Weren't you?"

"Which, as we know," Fred Barlow said distinctly, "Morell was not trying to do. So what?"

"Maybe we know it, sir, and maybe we don't. That isn't the point. It's no good sitting there shaking your head and saying, 'So what?'—like a film. Reminds me of the gentleman who used to own the judge's bungalow. Canadian gentleman, he was. Always so-whatting you even if you said it was a fine day."

Dr. Fell, who had been gazing absorbingly at something across the street, turned his head round and regarded the Inspector with instant attention.

"Do I understand you to say," he demanded, like one who cannot believe the good news his ears hear, "that the late owner of The Dunes was a Canadian?"

"You did."

"You're quite sure of that?"

"Of course I'm sure. Mr. Johnson, his name was. From Ottawa. His stuff's still all over the place. Why? Does it make any difference?"

"Does it make any difference!" exclaimed Dr. Fell. "That fact, and something which these bemused eyes of mine have just opened wide enough to notice, are the two most important things we have heard today. And I will tell you something else."

What this other point was Fred Barlow did not hear, though he would probably have made nothing of it if he had. A waiter put his head out on the balcony to say that Mr. Barlow was wanted on the telephone.

Fred took the call in Dr. Fell's bedroom.

"Is that you, Frederick?" said the judge's voice.

(He was 'Frederick' in private and 'Mr. Barlow' in public.)

"Yes, sir."

"I am given to understand," said Mr. Justice Ireton, "that Inspector Graham is lunching there. Is that correct?"

"Yes, he's here now."

"Then be good enough to give him a message from me. I have a visitor here now. A Mr. Appleby."

"Yes?"

"Mr. Appleby has just been telling me certain facts which lead him to believe that I killed the late lamented Anthony Morell. He has suggested that he and I keep this information to ourselves."

"So! Blackmail?"

The clear thin voice rasped.

"No, no. Nothing so crude. Mr. Appleby is at least a semi-respectable professional man. He merely suggested that he and I should be friends; and that a word or two of praise from me, dropped among my acquaintances, could do him much good. You perhaps hear him squawking in the background now?"

"Go on!"

"A most modest demand," said the cold voice. "But he will get no concessions from me. I do not succumb to anything remotely resembling intimidation. Kindly ask Inspector Graham to come over here. If I am able to hold my visitor here that long, the Inspector will then be able to hear the evidence against me from Mr. Appleby's own lips."

CHAPTER XIII

THEY FOUND MR. JUSTICE IRETON WAITING FOR THEM, sitting in his familiar easychair beside the chess table.

"I am sorry to tell you," he said, "that Mr. Appleby has left us. In something of a hurry, too."

No smile, malicious or otherwise, crossed the judge's face. He wore carpet-slippers, and his stout little body was buttoned up in an old-fashioned smoking-jacket which had nevertheless the air of being cut by a good tailor. He had removed his spectacles, though one finger still marked the place in the pages of the book he was reading.

"I could hardly have prevented him, you understand, even if I had been so enamoured of his company. Please sit down, gentlemen."

Inspector Graham looked at Fred Barlow, and Fred looked back at him.

It was getting on towards four o'clock in the afternoon, and turning chilly. The furniture and bilious blue-flowered wallpaper of the living-room had never seemed more dingy.

Of last night's occurrences, no trace now remained except the battered telephone. A small woolly rug had been tidily spread over the few traces of blood and sand in front of the desk.

Graham cleared his throat.

"Do you want to charge Mr. Appleby with attempted blackmail, sir?"

"Certainly not. I have nothing to charge him with in any case. He attempted no blackmail; he made no threats. He is a lawyer. So, unfortunately for him, am I."

"But if he's gone—?"

"That is all right," said the judge, making a slight gesture with his spectacles. "He may come to you presently, and tell you what he told me. Or he may not. I can't say. It depends on whatever it is he mistakes for his conscience. Meanwhile, it may save time if *I* tell you."

Graham pushed back the uniform-cap. Guileless as his reply sounded, Fred saw it for an attack in the one place where Graham knew it would work.

"Half a tick, sir, before you begin. Is Miss Ireton here, by any chance?"

The hand holding the spectacles stopped.

"No. Why should she be here?"

"Well, I took the liberty of sending Bert Weems over to Taunton to see her."

"So," said the judge. "It did not occur to you that the presence of a constable interrogating her in the midst of a house full of curious guests might be a trifle embarrassing for her?"

"Oh, that's all right, sir." Graham was reassuring. "This is Bert's afternoon off. He's in plain clothes. Smart-looking chap, too, when he's dressed up."

"Indeed."

"Yes. I thought it would look better. Even told him he could take his girl, in the sidecar of the motor-bike."

"And why did you send this gentleman to see my daughter?"

"Plenty of time for that, sir! We can come to that later," Graham declared briskly. "What was this story of Mr. Appleby's, now?"

The spectacles began to swing.

"As you like, Inspector. You heard Mr. Appleby's testimony last night."

"Yes?"

"This afternoon he chose to change it. Last night he made vague mention of certain vague remarks which he attributed to Mr. Morell, notably about a mysterious 'game' Mr. Morell contemplated playing on me; and said he had no notion of their meaning. This afternoon Mr. Appleby filled in the gaps.

"His story, in brief, is this. That Mr. Morell approached me pretending to be an extortionist. That he did this because he did not like my 'manner.' That he asked for three thousand pounds as the price of giving up my daughter. That I agreed to this sum. That we arranged to meet last night for the sum to be handed over. That Mr. Morell's purpose was to get me to name the largest amount I could conveniently pay, so that he could make a fool of me by handing over the same amount to me as a present to my daughter."

Graham seemed taken aback by sheer flat candour.

"So we've come to it at last!" he said.

"I don't follow you."

"The idea was to sort of teach you a lesson, eh?"

"That is Mr. Appleby's story. Unfortunately, it seems to have been Mr. Morell who received a lesson. So did Mr. Appleby."

"From the same person, sir?"

"No."

"Is the story true?"

"No."

"Not a word of it?"

"Not a word of it."

"Which one do you accuse of lying: Mr. Morell or Mr. Appleby?"

"Come, Inspector. Whether Morell invented the story and told it to Appleby, or Appleby invented the story for his own purpose and told it to me, I don't presume to say. That is for you to discover. All I can say is that no such conversation took place between Mr. Morell and me."

"For the love of God, sir, do you realize what you're letting yourself in for?"

"Let us have less melodrama, please. If you think I killed Mr. Morell, it's your duty to arrest me."

Gravely he folded up his spectacles, put them to mark the place in the book he had been reading, and laid down the book on the chess table.

"But I must warn you of the danger of accepting Mr. Appleby's 'testimony.' Told in court, such a tale would be ridiculed into outer darkness. I doubt whether in all human experience any man who honestly wanted to marry a girl has ever gone to her father and opened proceedings by saying that he would accept three thousand pounds to give her up."

"Mr. Morell was an Eyetalian."

"Still, I presume that even in Italy such an approach is not common. Let me continue. In the event that this were tried, what would happen? The girl's father would simply call in the girl and tell her about it. The suitor would then have to own up; and the matter would be over. Finally, let me remind you that you would have to prove this on the word of Mr. Appleby, a man already perjured, who only came forward with the story in an attempt to intimidate me in private. Can you be assured that jury would swallow it?"

"You're twisting it all up, sir!"

The pale eyebrows lifted.

"Oh? Where have I misstated any fact?"

"No, it's the *way* you put it! Look here, now. Can you honestly say you wanted that chap for a son-in-law?"

"Mr. Morell's manners were not Chesterfieldian. His clothes were regrettable. His mentality was negligible. But he had money, and he loved my daughter. I am a realist. Most jurymen, who usually have small incomes and marriageable daughters, will be realists too."

For a short time Graham appeared to ruminate.

Then he sat down on the edge of an easychair beyond the chess table. It was the same chair in which Morell had been sitting, about this time in the afternoon two days ago.

The afternoon was darker, full of leaden clouds edged with tarnished silver. Fred Barlow wished he had put on a sweater under his coat. As it was, he went across and closed the French window. It was not actually as cold as that; what they felt was the atmosphere of death.

"Do you know what I wish?" Graham asked suddenly. "I wish I could talk to you man to man."

"Well, why don't you?" The judge's voice was sharp. "Why can't you? Have I ever been accused of being a pompous fool or a stuffed shirt?"

"No, no. It's not that, exactly. But—!"

"Then out with it. Yes, you may speak in front of Mr. Barlow. Like my daughter, he has grown up under my eye. We are old acquaintances."

Graham brooded, his head lowered. He rubbed one hand heavily across the knuckles of the other, pressing them together. He shifted in his seat. Presently he lifted his head slightly, and peered up from under reddish eyebrows.

"I can't believe your story, sir. And that's a fact."

"Good. That's a beginning. Why can't you believe it? One other point, before you tell me!" This time a malicious smile did cross the judge's face. "Where is our friend Dr. Fell? I had hoped to see him here, when the attempt was made to put me in a corner."

"He'll be along presently. He couldn't move as fast as Mr. Barlow and me. Miss Tennant's driving him: and, anyway, he said he wanted to look at something on the way. And, so help me, I'm not trying to put you in a corner!"

"I beg your pardon. Go on."

Again Graham's right hand closed on the knuckles of the left.

"This Morell, now. *I* didn't like his looks any better than I bet you did…"

"Yes?"

"But let's take what happened last night. He gets here at twenty-five minutes past eight. He walks up and comes in by that window there." Graham nodded towards it. "Never mind *why* he was here. Never mind whether he was going to give you money, or expected to get it from you.

"Just suppose he comes in here, and finds the room empty. Now, what'd be the natural thing for him to do? Or for anybody to do? It'd be to call out, wouldn't it? It'd be to sing out and say, 'Hoy: is anybody at home?' Or go and see if anybody was at home. But you say you didn't see him come in, and didn't hear a sound of any kind."

"Correct."

Graham spoke with toiling lucidity.

"All right. Now, suppose somebody's following him. Suppose somebody follows him in through the window—to kill him. That could have happened. Maybe.

"But it'd be a pretty funny business. The murderer couldn't have walked in, had a row with him, and shot him. You'd have been bound to hear him in the kitchen. These walls are very thin, as I can testify for myself. You can easily hear somebody talking in another room."

(And as Fred Barlow could testify too.)

"Now, sir, Morell knew he was in danger. He was being threatened. Naturally, since he picked up the telephone and called for help. But even if he saw the murderer meant business—saw the gun, maybe—why did he go for the 'phone? Why didn't he call out for *you*; call out for a witness?

"And that's not all. Why did the murderer let him get as far as picking up the 'phone, ringing the exchange, getting a reply, and saying what he did, before the murderer went over and shot him from behind? Why didn't the murderer say, 'Keep your hands off that 'phone, or you'll get plugged now'? All of it hardly seems natural, like. The murderer couldn't have known but what Morell's first words might be, 'A man named Jones is going to shoot me. Help!' You see, sir?"

Graham held up his hand for silence, though Mr. Justice Ireton did not offer to speak.

"That's one side of it. Now I'll tell you straight, how we could get round that if *you* killed him."

"I am listening, Inspector."

"Morell comes up to the bungalow. He comes by the window because he looks through and sees you sitting in here—reading, maybe. Open; and in." Graham made a gesture. "You get up, and switch on the central lights. You ask him to sit down."

It had, Barlow thought, a devilish vividness. He could almost see the judge going through these motions, and Morell flashing white teeth in the opening of the window.

Graham went on:

"Maybe Morell says, continuing his joke, 'Well, have you raised the money?' You say, 'Yes. Just a minute, and I'll get it.' But you haven't got the money. You're all prepared to kill him instead. Somewhere, when you went to London that day, you got hold of an Ives-Grant ·32; I don't know where, but if we can trace it we'll have you.

"You go out of the room, saying you're going to get the money. Really to get the gun. Morell's sitting where I am now, with his back to the door. All of a sudden he realizes he's gone too far. He realizes you're up the pole and out to kill him. Yes, I know you've got a poker face! But murder's murder, in anybody's face; nasty, and hard to hide.

"I've got an idea he'd be pretty windy. Here he is, in the country half a mile from anybody, with a tough and unscrupulous old gent who won't give him a chance to explain; who'll just up and act, whatever he does. That's what you'd do, too, if I know you."

Twilight was deepening in the room.

"Wouldn't it be better to stick to facts?" suggested Barlow, for whom these suggestions were coming too close to his own imagination. "These flights of fancy—"

"Be quiet, Frederick," said the judge, shading his eyes with his hand. "Please go on, Inspector."

Graham gave an apologetic cough.

"Well, you understand now. Morell sees that 'phone. What he can do is ring up the exchange and say, 'I am speaking from The Dunes, Ireton's cottage. My name is Morell. I think there may be trouble here,' or something like that. Nothing *definite*, you see. Just enough to prevent you doing anything to him, in case you've got a mind to. Just to stop you, until he can explain to you.

"So he slips across to the 'phone."

Graham paused, and got to his feet. By way of illustration, he walked over to the desk. The desk lamp, with an immovable bronze-metal shade, stood at the back of the blotter. Graham pulled its chain and switched it on. It made a brilliant circle of light round the desk, leaving everything else in gloom.

Adjusting the desk chair, Graham sat down in it. His back was now towards them. The telephone was at his right hand.

"He comes over here quietly," the Inspector went on, "and he speaks quietly. Whispers, even. The door"—Graham glanced over his right shoulder—"the door is behind him, in the wall on his right. He can't see it without turning.

"He rings the exchange, and says, 'The Dunes. Ireton's cottage.' He gets just that far when he glances over his shoulder, like this. He sees the door opening. He sees what you've got in your hand. He whirls back to the 'phone and shouts, '*Help*.' He's got no time to say anything else before you've taken one—two—three—quick steps, and let him have it behind the right ear."

There was silence.

In imagination, Fred Barlow heard the shot.

But he heard nothing in actuality until Graham creaked round in the swivel-chair, turning it to face them.

"That's how it could have happened, sir. You'll excuse me for all these goings-on. Acting it out. But I wanted to see it. And damn me if I *don't* see it."

Graham's face was lowering and dogged. Mr. Justice Ireton nodded, as though he saw the force of this reconstruction. But there was a wrinkle between his brows.

"Inspector," he said, "you disappoint me."

"Oh, I don't claim to be any Sherlock Holmes, sir! I'm just a country copper with a lot of trouble on my hands. All the same—"

"That was not what I meant. I meant that I never thought you had such a low opinion of my intelligence."

"Pardon?"

"If I were really going to commit a murder, do you in all honesty think I should ever go about it as clumsily as that? Do you?"

The judge seemed genuinely interested. He fished his spectacles out of the book, and put them on.

"By your analysis, this crime was not committed on the

spur of the moment. It was planned. I had at least twenty-four hours in which to plan it.

"I had invited this man to my house. I procured a revolver. I shot him here. I sat down, holding the weapon, and waited for you to come and take me. I constructed a story which, if it were a lie, a child of six could have made more convincing. Yet I am an old campaigner, wily in the ways of evidence." He blinked his eyes, and blinked them again. "Do I really strike you as being so anxious to get myself hanged?"

A long shadow fell across the last light from the windows.

For what length of time that shadow had been there nobody could tell, for no one noticed it until it moved. Dr. Gideon Fell, who seemed to have been looking at something in the region of the ceiling, turned the handle of one window and blundered in. He breathed hard, and his air was one of powerful embarrassment.

"You are late," said Mr. Justice Ireton.

"Yes. I—er—fear so."

"We have just been reconstructing the crime. Would you care to join us?"

"No, thanks." The doctor's voice was hurried. "I have seen what I care to see. Er—Inspector. There's a young constable down at the gate, in a great state of mysteriousness and agitation, who asks if he can have a word with you in private."

"Bert Weems?"

"The chap who was here last night: yes. Mr. Barlow, Miss Tennant has gone home. She asked me to tell you not to forget the Esplanade Hotel swimming-party tonight. Oh, Inspector. One other thing. When you searched this room, you didn't find any chewing-gum anywhere, did you?"

"Any *what*, sir?"

"Chewing-gum," returned Dr. Fell, champing his jaws by way of illustration, but with so serious a face that they all refrained from comment.

"No chewing-gum. No."

"No," said Dr. Fell slowly, "I didn't think you would. I won't intrude on you any longer. I am going to try the unheard-of experiment of walking home. Cheer-o."

They stared after him as he lumbered away down the lawn.

Inspector Graham seemed to be on thorns.

"Excuse me half a minute," he said to the others. "I'll just see what Bert wants."

He hurried out into the twilight, which swallowed him up, and the window remained open. Dimly, above the rush of the sea, they could hear the thud-thud-pop from the engine of a stationary motor cycle down in the road.

Mr. Justice Ireton, his hands folded over his stomach, sat so quietly that Fred was startled to hear the urgent note in his voice when he spoke.

"That will be the well-dressed gentleman whom Graham sent to Taunton. Frederick, would you like to do me a favour?"

"Naturally, if I can."

"You have a step like a Red Indian. And the light is dim. See whether you can get close enough to hear what they are saying, without being observed yourself. For God's sake do not question my orders. Go."

It was one of the few times in his life he had ever heard Horace Ireton use a scriptural expletive.

Fred Barlow went through the bungalow, out by the kitchen door, and round the side of the house. The sandy soil muffled his footsteps. Skirting the fence at one side, he made for the road in front.

PC Weems's police motor cycle, with (empty) sidecar, had been drawn up at the gate. Weems, with one foot on the ground, was addressing Graham and Dr. Fell. They could not see Fred at the angle outside the fence. But, since they had to raise their voices above the popping of the engine, he could hear them distinctly.

"Inspector," was the first word he heard, "Inspector, *we've got 'em.*"

"What do you mean, got 'em?" roared Graham. "What are you talking about?"

"Listen, Inspector. You sent me over to see Miss Ireton. Nothing in it, like. You'd just forgotten to ask whether she could identify the revolver. So you sent me to do it. You said I could take my girl along. Remember?"

"I remember. What about it?"

"Well, listen, Inspector. My girl is Florence Swan, from the telephone exchange."

"I know she is. And you tell her from me that if she rings you up at the station again, when you're on duty—"

"Now, wait, Inspector. Wait! Miss Ireton couldn't identify the gun. But Florence identified *her*. Florence identified her voice."

"Eh?"

"Listen. Last night, about ten minutes before the 'help' call came through from the bungalow, Florence took another call. It was from a woman, 'phoning from a public callbox, who wanted to put through a toll-call without having any money."

"Well? And shut that blinking motor off, can't you?"

Weems did so. Stillness, except for the wash of the sea, descended with drowsy calm. And Weems's voice rose up through it.

"The callbox," he said, "was the one in Lovers' Lane—over three hundred yards from here. Up on the old building estate, by the model houses. You know there's a callbox there?"

"Yes."

"There's no doubt about the place, because when this young lady said she wanted to put through a toll-call to Taunton, Florence said, '*What is your number, please?*' The young lady said, 'Tawnish 1818.' Which is right. I've just been up to see."

Graham's big figure looked suddenly alert.

"Go on, Bert," he said.

"Ah!" Weems drew a breath of satisfaction. "It took four minutes to get the call through to Taunton. Then Florence said, '*Here is your party. Deposit fivepence, please. Then press Button A and speak.*' The young lady went clear up in the air. Florence said she'd already sounded all wild and dithery, but now was worse. She said she'd come out without her purse, and hadn't got any money. She said wouldn't Florence just put the call through, and they'd pay at the other end.

"Florence tried to explain she couldn't do that. Florence tried to explain that unless you put the money in, you couldn't press Button A and the connection wouldn't work. The young lady wouldn't believe her. She seemed to think all Florence had to do was pull a lever or something, and the call would go through.

"The result was, they had a hell of a slanging-match which

went on for more than three minutes before Florence rang off. Inspector, the number that young lady wanted to ring was Taunton 34955: Miss Tennant's house. And the young lady was Miss Constance Ireton."

Weems stopped for breath.

Inspector Graham glanced at Dr. Fell, and both were eloquently silent. It was Weems who explained.

"Now, look, Inspector. Miss Ireton first rang the exchange at twenty minutes past eight—"

Graham found his voice.

"Is your Florence sure of that? *Sure*, now?"

"She's charted it, Inspector. They're bound to."

"Go on."

"It took four minutes to get the call through to Taunton. Then three minutes and over while she and Florence were arguing. That means it was eight-twenty when Miss Ireton went into the callbox, and eight twenty-seven at the earliest before she left it. That callbox in Lovers' Lane is a good three hundred yards from this bungalow."

"It is," agreed Graham grimly.

"Ah! And yet look at what she tells us! She says she was here in front of the bungalow all that time. Sir, she couldn't 'a' been! She couldn't 'a' seen any of the things she says she did. The most she could 'a' done would have been to walk back here—by the main road, or maybe the back path—just about in time to hear the shot fired at half past eight."

Weems broke off. His voice was full of an almost reproachful wonder.

"That young lady's lying," he added. "That young lady's lying!"

Inspector Graham nodded.

"Bert," he said, "you never said a truer word. You'll never say a truer word, until you come to testify at the trial. That young lady's lying."

CHAPTER XIV

"JACK-KNIFE," CALLED THE FAIR-HAIRED YOUNG MAN, as soon as his head emerged above water. He flung the wet hair out of his eyes.

Hoots of derision echoed back hollowly from the walls.

"That's not a jack-knife, you ass," yelled somebody. "A jack-knife dive is when you bend double and touch your toes in midair, and then straighten out before you hit the water. What you did was a kind of a jitterbug-twist that didn't mean anything at all."

"I tell you it was a jack-knife," the young man said truculently. His face was red. He tried to haul himself up by the rail round the inside edge of the pool, and slopped back again.

A girl in a red bathing-suit intervened with pacifying smoothness.

"All right, dear. It was a jack-knife. Come and have a drink."

"Ah! Now you're talking!" said the athlete. "Best bloody jack-knife I ever did," he added, blowing bubbles from the surface of the water.

The vault which houses the swimming-pool at the Esplanade Hotel is some eighty feet long, and proportionately broad and high. Its walls are made of smooth-fitted panels of looking-glass, its floor is of marble mosaic. Its water, greenish-tinted, makes the white tiles of the pool waver and tremble with continuous motion. And the floor-space round the pool is considerable; for it is used as a lounge, with bright-coloured beach-chairs and tables lining the mirror walls.

From here, wide-open double-doors lead into the American bar, a smallish room presenting a vista of vivid bottles behind a bar-counter of frosted glass. Another door in the same wall leads to an underground conservatory, artificially lighted and heated. The management are tolerant, the waiters swift. In fine, any person already primed with cocktails could desire no more ideal place for a beano.

Something like this was in progress at half past nine, when Fred Barlow arrived.

Thirteen guests, seven women and six men, sat or lounged or swam or fell in. These ranged from the very young man with the taste for fancy diving to a middle-aged lady, a remote courtesy-aunt of Jane's, who was supposed to be "keeping an eye on" the house-party and on whom a close eye had to be kept by Jane herself. The girls' bathing-dresses were of all colours, and all different. Nor were they conspicuous for prudery. Some guests wore beach-robes of heavy towelling; but this was not observable in the case of any girl with a good figure.

Fred, stepping into the clean, close, tangy atmosphere, was dazed by noises. Voices and echoes: from the echo of laughter to the fine, hollow echo of a splash. Voices struck at him.

"Tony ought to be here," said a lean, alcoholic-looking blonde in a blue-striped robe.

"Poor old Tony!"

"Sh-h!"

"It's all right. Connie's not here. She wouldn't come."

"Waiter! Coo-ee! *Wai*ter!"

"Like to see me do a swan-dive now?"

"No, dear."

"I do so like to see young people enjoying themselves," said Jane's aunt. "In my—*gup!* Pardon me, my dear—in my day, it was all so different."

The mingling of voices and echoes rolled over him. He was very conscious of his street-clothes. Then he saw Jane.

She saw him at the same time, and came towards him. She was wearing a yellow bathing-suit. The effect was inspiring. She had just come out of the water; she also wore a yellow rubber bathing-cap which she took off to shake out her hair, and caught up a beach-robe from a chair. She had pulled this round herself by the time he had reached her.

"I'm sorry I'm late," he said.

"What's that, Fred?"

"I said I'm sorry I'm late," he yelled above the din.

"Oh! That's all right. You said you might be, but I thought you weren't coming. Have you had any dinner?"

He reflected. "Yes. Yes, I think so. A sandwich or something. Jane, I don't want to be a killjoy; but can I see you alone for a minute?"

"Not trouble again?"

"Bad trouble, I'm afraid."

She hesitated.

"You look worried to death," she said. "Can't it wait for five minutes? Why not have a drink and take a turn in the pool first? It'll do you good."

The prospect was inviting. He could both stretch and relax. And he had brought his kit along.

"Do!" she urged. "I'll get you a drink while you're changing. The dressing-rooms are out in the hall you came in by. You'll see the sign."

"Right."

As he changed he reflected, though he was on the lean side and no ruddy Apollo, still there was nothing wrong with his shoulders and it would be long before he had a stomach.

Jane was awaiting him with gin-and-French when he returned. He drank, and felt better; not much, but more human. He said abruptly:

"Where's Connie? She's not here. I heard somebody say so."

"No, she wouldn't come. She's at my house; probably gone to bed. If you've come just to see her. I'm afraid your luck's out."

"She's not at your house," he said. "We don't know where she is. The police are still looking for her."

"The police?"

"Yes. Excuse me a moment."

There were two diving-boards, a high one at the top of a ladder and another a little above water-level. Fred chose the lower one, and left it in a dive that would make him stretch. He felt the creak and snap of the board as its edge released him; the soar of motion, open and shut and open; then the exhilaration and balance of the straight, deep drop, heels not too far over, as the water closed round him.

The water felt cool and grateful. He turned up his hands and floated through a green twilight, which drew out wavering lines of white tiles. Feeling soothed and almost drowsy, he floated to the surface and struck out for the rail with slow, lazy, overarm strokes.

He had almost reached it when he was astonished to hear the clamour that seemed to have broken out.

"*That* was a jack-knife!"

"What was?"

"That! What that fellow just did."

A pink and truculent face appeared over Fred's head, peering down at him.

"Like to see me do a one-and-a-half?" it leered. "High board," it added.

"Hugo," said a girl in a red bathing-suit, "don't be an ass. You'll break your silly neck."

Hugo, whoever he might be, instantly climbed the ladder to the high spring-board.

"One-and-a-half," he announced—and hurled himself into the air.

What complicated manoeuvre he thought he was performing was perhaps not even clear to himself, and certainly not to the spectators. The only question in anybody's mind was whether he would land flat on his face or flat on his back. They were not long left in doubt. He landed flat on his face, with a hollow, thocking splash which flung spray as far as the mirror walls. It drew from several of the watchers a howl of joy which presently changed to a silence of consternation.

Hugo floated gently just below the surface; face downwards, but turning over on his side. He did not move except with the motion of the water. There was no sound in the big hall until a fat girl screamed.

A hairy-chested young pianist plunged in and dragged him out. They laid him dripping on the dripping mosaic floor, and put down their drinks to gather round him. There was a broad reddish mark on his forehead.

"He's all right," a voice announced with relief. "Just knocked out, the silly ass. His forehead hit the water. Get him some brandy."

Jane's aunt moaned and showed the extent of her Christian charity by giving up her own brandy.

"Don't you think we ought to throw some water over him?" asked the fat girl.

This was considered a good idea, so they scooped up handfuls out of the pool and sloshed him down again.

Jane and Fred were some distance away from the others. The latter, towelling his face and head, glanced sideways at Jane. She was sitting in a beach-chair, her robe thrown back, her hands on her knees, her face a picture of misery. He had never seen the capable, competent Jane Tennant look like that; he had not known she could feel like that.

"I never bring luck to anybody, do I?" asked Jane.

He could understand. The white, limp face of the unconscious boy on the floor brought back to his mind the memory of another white, limp face.

"Let's get out of here," he said.

"Yes," said Jane fiercely. "Yes, yes, yes, yes!"

She slipped into sandals. And, since all the others were still arguing round Hugo, nobody—a fact which was later to prove of importance—noticed them go.

Pulling on his own robe, he led the way round the pool and opened the glass door leading to the conservatory. Once inside, Jane hesitated again.

"Do you think I ought to leave them?"

"The bar and pool won't close until eleven o'clock. It's not ten yet. They'll be all right. There are one or two things I've *got* to talk to you about. Two things in particular. Come on."

The conservatory was very long and rather narrow, divided into sections by wall-panels and doors of opaque coloured glass. Its atmosphere was heavy with the closeness of plants and ferns, its floor also of marble mosaic. He led the way through to the last section, and closed the door. Screened round by banks of ferns, there were some wicker chairs, a table, and a bench in the little open space.

Neither of them sat down.

"Yes?" asked Jane. "What are these two things you've got to talk about?"

"The first is Connie. We've got to find her before the police do. Do you think she's gone back to London?"

"I don't know, but I shouldn't think so. There's no train, and we're using all the cars. Why? Why must we find her?"

"Jane, she's been telling a pack of lies. And they've found out about it."

"What lies?"

"Wait. Now tell me. Were you at home last night about twenty-five minutes past eight?"

"Why do you ask that?" Her voice was sharp.

"That's part of it. Were you?"

"No, I was on my way to see Dr. Fell. Why?"

"Because Connie tried to put through a 'phone-call to your

house from a callbox in a place called Lovers' Lane—some distance away from the judge's bungalow. The operator claims to have got somebody at the other end. If they can prove that call was to your house, and that it was Connie speaking, she's in an ugly position. You don't remember anything about a call, do you?"

"Not to take it, no. But, now I remember it, Annie did say this morning that there'd been a call from Tawnish that never got through."

"So!"

"But, Fred, that means…?"

"Yes. Connie couldn't have been outside the bungalow at twenty-five minutes past eight, or anywhere near there. She couldn't have seen Morell arrive. She's lying; and they're suspicious enough of the judge already. This may tip the balance."

"I see," Jane said slowly. She looked up. "What was the other thing you wanted to talk about?"

They faced each other more like duellists than friends.

It was very quiet in the little enclosure; with a warm, heavy oppressive quiet. The lights, of such dull pale white that they seemed bluish, only intensified it. They were shut away in a little corner, out of the world, behind plants and opaque coloured glass.

"This," he said, "is the other thing."

He walked up to her. He put his arm over her shoulder and round her left side. He tilted her head back and kissed her, very hard, on the lips.

CHAPTER XV

SHE RESPONDED, BUT ONLY PERFUNCTORILY, AS ONE WHO fulfils a social duty. Her hands remained at his shoulders, pressed flat there. After a moment she pushed him away, drew her head back, and looked him in the eyes with steady appraisal.

She said quietly:

"Why did you do that?"

He spoke, or tried to speak, just as calmly.

"Because I'm in love with you. You may as well know that now as later."

"Are you? Or do you only think you are?"

"*Oh, God, Jane!*"

"What about Connie?"

"I think I worked it out last night. I've never been in love with Connie. Connie's—gone."

"Just when she needs you?"

He dropped his hands, moved back, and walked round the table. He rapped his knuckles on the table; first quietly, and then with increasing violence.

"I don't take back any of that. I'm very fond of Connie. I'll still fight her battles; I'll still fetch and carry for her. But it's not the same thing. This is different. You don't know how different. That's all. Sorry if I've offended you."

"Offended me?" said Jane, her face blazing. "Offended me!" She stretched out her hands to him. "Come here, my dear. Come here to me for a moment."

He looked at her, and then moved round the table. Both of them were breathing rapidly. It was a contrast to their low-voiced, studied, almost muttering speech. But, when he touched her hand, and put his arm across her shoulder again, the mood changed to one charged with violence.

Some five minutes later, Jane said breathlessly:

"You know, this is positively indecent."

"Do you mind?"

"No. But if one of the hotel people should—"

"Ho! Let 'em!"

Five minutes later, when, in a manner neither could afterwards recall, they found themselves sitting on the wicker bench, Jane disengaged herself and sat back.

"This must stop. Sit over there. Please! I mean it."

"But if you—"

"Anywhere. Any time," said Jane. "Always. For ever. But don't you *see*—" She pressed her hands on her forehead. "I feel I'm being a beast to Connie somehow. I know I'm not, really, and yet that's what I feel."

This sobered him somewhat.

"And now she's in trouble," Jane went on. "Why? Only through trying to shield her father. That's decent of her, if you like. Fred, we *can't*. Not while she's… No, sit where you are. Give me a cigarette."

There was a packet of cigarettes in the pocket of his beach-robe. His hand shook when he took them out, and fumblingly struck a match. Her cheeks were bright with colour, but her own hand was steady as she accepted cigarette and light.

"Fred, I've got a confession to make too. *I* can identify that revolver."

He shook out the match, and dropped it on the floor.

"That is," she corrected herself, "I haven't actually identified it to the police yet, but I'm positive it's the same one. It's the Ives-Grant ·32 that poor Cynthia Lee used on Morell five years ago."

He stared at her.

"But the Lee girl wouldn't—that is—?"

"No: I don't think Cynthia did it, just because of the revolver. You see, it's not in her possession. Before the trial it was whisked away by a man named Hawley, Sir Charles Hawley. He 'hid' it by putting it in a huge collection of guns he's got all over the walls of his flat, where nobody ever noticed it."

She broke off, for her companion's expression was curious. He spoke with painful clearness.

"Did you say Sir Charles Hawley?"

"Yes."

"Who has since been made a judge? Mr. Justice Hawley?"

"That's right."

"When he went to London yesterday," said Fred, fashioning the syllables carefully, "Horace Ireton had lunch with his old friend, Sir Charles Hawley, at Hawley's flat. He told Inspector Graham that last night."

There was a silence.

"The crafty old devil!" muttered Fred, with a growing comprehension not untinged with admiration. "He pinched that gun out of old Hawley's flat. Hawley was Cynthia Lee's counsel at the trial, wasn't he? I remember now. Don't you see the beauty of the scheme? Horace Ireton doesn't care how much they try to trace that revolver. Even if they do trace it to Sir Charles Hawley—even if they do—Hawley will have to swear that it doesn't come from his collection and that he never saw it before, because *he* can't admit he was unlawfully in the possession of evidence he unlawfully suppressed at the Lee trial."

Fred paused, and added:

"The crafty old devil!"

"You know, my dear, I'm rather afraid you've got it."

He whirled round. "You haven't told anybody else about this, have you?"

"Yes. I—I told Dr. Fell, before I'd even heard Morell was dead. That is, I described Cynthia's revolver."

She repeated, in some detail, the account she had given Dr. Fell last night.

"But I still don't quite understand," she concluded, drawing her robe more tightly round her. "Even if Sir Charles won't identify it, suppose somebody else does? Cynthia herself, for instance? Or me?"

"Could you *swear* to the revolver?"

"N-no."

"Wasn't the defence at the Lee trial that no such revolver had ever existed?"

"Yes."

"Well, Cynthia Lee can't come out now and say, 'Yes, that's the gun I used five years ago.' And neither can you, unless you want to rake up more trouble for her. Sir Charles Hawley would only say you were all dotty anyway. No. Horace Ireton is protected at every point of the compass. They'll never even guess where he pinched it."

"I think Dr. Fell guesses, though."

Fred brooded. "If he does, he certainly hasn't mentioned it to Graham. Which is another problem. If he guesses, why is he holding his hand?"

"Perhaps because he still doesn't think the judge is guilty. Do *you* think so?"

"Against all the dictates of reason," replied Fred, after a pause, "against all the dictates of common sense—no, I don't."

He got to his feet. He stood in front of her, and looked down at her.

Her eyes had a strained, happy wildness; her lips were half smiling. But when he attempted to take her hands, she drew away.

"Can't we forget all this?" he said.

"No. You know we can't. Not for a minute. No! No! No! I won't!"

"It took a lot of time to find you, Jane."

"There's a lot of time ahead of us."

"I wonder."

"Why do you say that?" she asked quickly.

Drifting, never very far away since last night, the black patch that could cloud his mind returned again. Since then it seemed to have spread like ink. It swallowed him up. It was all the worse now, because Jane was so near.

"This appears to be the hour of the confessional," he told her. "So perhaps I'd better make my confession."

She smiled. "If it's about any other love-affairs—"

"No. Nothing like that. Jane, I think I may have killed a man last night."

The thick, warm stillness of the conservatory grew to a roaring in their ears. He stood looking down at her, his eyes fixed and unsmiling. To Jane, who was utterly happy, the words came first without comprehension; and then, as he nodded, like a blow under the heart.

She moistened her lips.

"Not—?"

"No." His voice sounded firm: the slow, pleasant baritone he could make ring with sincerity in court. "Not Morell. That's not on my conscience, anyhow."

"Then who?"

"Black Jeff. I ran over him in my car."

She half got up, but sank down again.

"That tramp?"

"Yes. I told Graham something about it today. But I didn't tell him all of it."

Jane hastily reached down and ground out her cigarette on the marble floor. Then, drawing her robe round her and her legs up under her, she faced him with all the strength of sympathy in her nature. His expression was cryptic; for the first time she did not understand him; she felt rather afraid of him.

"So that," she murmured, "that was why you were looking so queer at lunch when they were asking you about it!"

"You noticed it?"

"I notice anything that concerns you, Fred. Tell me. What happened?"

He made a gesture.

"Well, Jeff came staggering out of Lovers' Lane and fell straight in front of my car—"

"It was an accident, then?"

"Yes. Oh, I'm not in great danger of going to prison, if that's what you mean. But listen. I got out, and examined him, and carted him across to the other side of the road; just as I said. I went back to my car to get a torch, just as I said. And, also, as I said, when I returned with the torch he was gone."

"But, my dear Fred! If the man was badly hurt, he surely didn't get up and walk away. He couldn't have been badly hurt."

He spoke quietly.

"Don't ask me to go into details now. They're not pleasant. All I can say is this. I *know*, from evidence I saw myself, that poor old Jeff had an injury few people could survive. I was going to tell the good PC Weems, of course, when he came pelting up on his bike. In fact, I started to. But he started in to tell me about the other business—"

"And that drove it out of your head?"

"Yes. So, as far as I'm concerned, I let Jeff go away and die without stopping him, and without telling anyone about it. I still haven't told anyone about it. Coldly and candidly, I don't mean to; and I would defy the Recording Angel to prove it against me in open court. But it was a hell of a thing to do. You get nightmares."

"Well?" asked Jane, after a pause.

"Well, what?"

"Don't you feel better?" said Jane, smiling.

He drew the sleeve of his beach-robe across his forehead. "Yes, you know—by the Lord, I do!"

"Sit down beside me," she said. "You want someone to talk to. Harangue. You're so absorbing the Ireton training that in a few more years you'd be stuffed like that moose's head in the judge's room. You say this Black Jeff got up and walked away; and *I* say he *couldn't* have been much hurt. Are you even sure your car hit him?"

He turned rather excitedly. "That's the funny part. First off, I could have sworn I hadn't. But then, afterwards, when I saw—"

"Being here," said Jane, "you might kiss me."

Presently, drawing a deep breath, Fred sat back and assumed a rather dictatorial air.

"The English Sunday," he declared, "has been for many years mocked and maligned. Its dullness has been a target for more cheap wit than any institution except mothers-in-law and the Royal Academy. This misconception, I say, is monstrous. I am going to write an essay and expose it. If this particular Sunday night has been dull, my beloved, then all I can observe, with due moderation..."

He paused, for she had sat up straight.

"Sunday!" she exclaimed.

"Correct. What about it?"

"Sunday!" said Jane. "The bar and swimming-pool aren't closed at eleven o'clock. They're closed at ten. All the attendants lock up. And it must be nearly eleven now!"

He whistled.

"So all your guests," he observed, not without satisfaction, "must have been chased away home long ago? Well, well."

"But, Fred, my dear, if we can't get our clothes—"

"Personally, my witch (yes, I said witch), it is a prospect which fails to curdle my blood. I see no urgent necessity for more clothes than we are wearing now. Contrariwise, as someone remarked; but that by the way."

"Go home like this?"

"Never mind. We'll rout somebody out. Come on."

As he thought back over it, he did not remember seeing lights in other parts of the conservatory for some time. He pushed open the opaque-glass door into the next section.

Darkness.

All the other doors were open through the long length of the conservatory, and darkness made it ghostly. Down at the end, in the direction of the swimming hall, shone a vague glimmer of light.

They groped through, their faces brushed by unpleasantly fuzzy tentacles from the plants, and emerged into the hall beside the pool. Only one small light, up in the centre of the big domed roof, was now burning; presumably it was left on all night.

Its reflection showed in pin-points from the dim, darkening mirrors. It trembled on the faintly agitated water of the pool, opaque green. It blurred the outline of beach-chairs and tables, veiling them with shadows. Everything looked neat, swept, cold, and slightly sinister. The doors to the American bar were shut and locked.

Fred tried the big door which led out into the hall: to the dressing-rooms and the way upstairs. It was locked too.

"That's done it," he said aloud.

The sound of his voice rose up and rolled back at them hollowly in the marble shell. A distinct echo muttered, 'That's done it,' from one side of the dome.

Jane began to laugh, which was repeated with grotesque effect by a sly voice from the dome.

"You mean we can't get out?"

"We can try banging on the door. But this room is underground; and it's out of season at the hotel, which means a skeleton staff; and in the mysterious city of Tawnish they go to bed early. However, here goes."

He tried banging on the heavy door and shouting. After five steady minutes of it he had achieved no result except such an unnerving din of echoes that Jane begged him to stop.

They looked at each other.

Jane's eyes twinkled. "Well, I suppose there are worse places," she sighed. "Still, it does seem a pity on our very *first* evening."

"Anywhere with you, my witch, were paradise enow. But I have strong romantic objections to us dossing down either on a marble floor or among a mess of evergreens. Hold on!" He reflected.

"I was just wondering."

"Yes?"

"Why was that light left on in the place where we were? Not out of consideration for us. For the same reason this one was: an all-night light. Got it! That's the farthest end of the conservatory. I seem to remember there's a door there. *If* it's open, it leads to a staircase and to the main lounge upstairs at the back."

"Shall we try it?"

"I will try it. You stay here. In spite of what I said, I am not going to have you parading through the main hall of the Esplanade Hotel in that outfit. If the door does happen to be open, I'll go up and down and let you out by this one here in two shakes."

"All right. Don't be long."

He hurried into the conservatory, his blue robe flying. After a difficult passage through, to judge by the language, there was a long pause and then a triumphant shout.

"Open! Back straight away!"

Distantly, the door closed.

Jane drew a deep breath of relief.

As though the closing of the door had set up vibrations all through the conservatory, the water in the pool seemed to tremble. The reflection of that one dim light split up into glints on imperceptible waves. Even her cork beach sandals made an audible sound on this floor.

She sat down in a deckchair pushed back against the wall, and stretched back in it. Her bathing-suit felt clammy under the robe; she wanted dry clothes.

One part of her mind told her that she did not like this place at all. Even the sight of your own reflection, caught out of the tail of the eye as you moved, had a stealthy suggestion; it was as though people were coming at you, in all directions, out of dim rooms beyond the mirrors. Yet the other part of her mind, the wide-awake part, was fiercely exultant. She half closed her eyes as she contemplated the roof.

"You," she prayed. "You, Who grant prayers: I'm happy.

All my life I've felt dead, but now I'm alive. Make him happy too. That's all I want. Make—"

Jane stopped, and sat up straight.

Without warning, the light in the dome went out.

CHAPTER XVI

Jane sat still.

Her first thought was that the person responsible must be Fred, switching off this light under the impression that he was switching others on. But this hardly seemed reasonable; and she was a reasonable person. It wasn't likely that a panel controlling the pool-lights would be out in a hall clear at the other end of the conservatory. It was much more likely to be outside the main door here.

Which might mean that there was somebody out in the passage now, if she called through the door.

Sudden darkness is at any time startling. Here it was catastrophic. Jane got up, and realized she had only the haziest idea in which direction the door lay.

Darkness seemed more than a mere bandage across her eyes: it was a thick weight piled upon her. She felt a touch of panic, the sensation of being lost, which is experienced sometimes in dreams. To darkness was added that earlier quality of underground silence, completing a tomb.

"Hello!" she called.

Her own voice made the shell ring; it seemed to slip round that sounding-board like water in a bowl. The echo gurgled, "Hello" from the dome, and then the vibration quivered away. She took an experimental step forward. She kicked off her sandals, because they made a noise that bothered her, and took another step.

Where was the door? Where was the pool, even? Better not take too many steps, or she might walk over the edge of it. She turned towards her left, groping on ahead; but this only served to confuse directions still more.

Where was Fred? Why didn't he come?

She started to walk boldly forward in what she thought was the right direction. After two steps she stopped short, and stood bent forward, rigidly, listening.

There was somebody in here with her.

The sound was soft, but unmistakable. It was the faint drag and shuffle of leather-soled shoes—starting, stopping, starting again—as someone moved towards her: uncertainly, trying to find out where she was.

"*Who's there?*"

The sound instantly stopped. Her voice had gone up; the echoes were shrill, and seemed to rain round her, clattering at her ears. But no reply came except the repetition of her words from the dome. After many seconds, after the echoes had died away and some other person seemed to be listening too, those shuffling footsteps began again.

They had come much nearer now.

Under her feet the marble mosaic felt warm and faintly ridged. Her heart was thudding, and she had come close to the edge of blind panic. It seemed to her that she had been shut up here for hours. She was being tracked, quietly; being pressed and edged into a narrower corner or a smaller tomb. Each time she spoke, it gave the tracker his directions and brought him closer.

Jane backed away, with no notion of where she was going. Her foot struck the edge of a light beach-chair, which rattled. She groped for it, picked it up, and at random flung it into the darkness ahead of her. It clattered on the floor, and slithered for some distance.

Then she turned and ran, checking herself as she slipped and almost fell; one foot on the smooth, curved surface of a void like a gulf.

The pool.

She would be safe in the pool. She was an excellent swimmer; more at home in the water than almost anyone she knew. She could take her chances there. And at least it would resolve her doubts. If the other person tried to follow her there, it would be a sure sign that—

As she stood on the edge of the pool, she could hear her own hard, harsh breathing, the accent of terror. It drowned out any other sound. She prayed that she was standing straight, standing at the deep end of the pool. She slipped out of her robe and tossed it aside. She poised herself and dived.

The shock of the splash went up in hollow thunder. To Jane, sliding down through interminable depths, the water seemed colder: icy cold. She hadn't her cap on, she remembered. She would look a sight when Fred came back. If Fred ever did come back.

Two long breast-strokes took her to the bottom of the

pool. About six or seven feet deep here. But this was worse than ever; this was like being buried. She swam up to the surface, shook her head out of water, and listened.

Nothing. Nothing, for a long time, except the slap of disturbed water against tile. Her hair was streaming, and she pushed it out of her eyes. She could not help gasping for breath, though she hoped she could not be heard. Treading water, she strained her ears in desperation.

Nothing.

Her arms moved and wove, automatically, to help in keeping her afloat. After long shuddering breaths, she felt again the necessity to go—go anywhere—keep on the move. She slid out almost silently, with the side-stroke. The water was colder yet, or seemed so. After half a dozen strokes she sensed rather than saw or felt the white porcelain rail inside the edge of the pool. She grasped it, shuddering and trying to slow down her breath. She waited, listening.

There was another sound.

A gloved hand descended on hers, and fingers closed round her wrist.

Jane's screams were instinctive. They frightened her as much as the hand, for she saw her reason cracking. They went piercing up to the domed roof, filling the hall before they were echoed. But, even as she screamed, she kicked backwards by instinct with her heels against the white tiles of the side. Something seemed to flash past her shoulder and burn her.

The grip of the fingers was torn loose. Jane shot backwards, turning sideways and choking as her head splashed under water. Then she became aware of several things happening at once. She heard quick, running footsteps: which even at that time made her wonder. Somebody began to rattle and bang at what must be the door to the hall. There were voices.

Every light over the swimming-pool flashed on, tier following tier, until it was as bright as day. There were more voices, and she heard the grating of a key in a lock.

The door to the hall opened. Fred Barlow, followed by a sleepy-looking night-porter in his shirt-sleeves, burst in and stopped short. Otherwise, the gaudy hall was empty.

In his turn, Fred saw the agitated swimming-pool with water slopping over its edges and gleaming across the floor. He saw Jane stare back at him, after which she began to swim as though with over-tired arms towards the little ladder leading up from the pool to the floor.

The figure in the yellow bathing-suit grasped at the rails of the ladder, and had difficulty in pulling itself up. She emerged at the top, her knees a little bent, gasping but trying to laugh.

He found his voice.

"What is it?" he shouted. "For God's sake what happened?"

"S-somebody tried to—"

He put his arms round the dripping figure, pushed back the wet hair from her face, and made incoherent noises which were intended to be soothing.

"Tried to what?"

"I don't know. Kill me, I thought. I look an awful sight, don't I?" She coughed. "Get me my robe, will you?"

It was the night-porter who handed her the robe. While she put it on, laughing, and combing back her hair with her fingers, and assuring them she was all right, the night-porter stood by with an expression of heavy, pained disapproval. He seemed to say that broadmindedness was broadmindedness, but that this was carrying matters too far. Even when Jane told her story his expression did not change.

"There's nobody here now, miss," he pointed out.

Fred's face was white. "Whoever did it," he said, "could have gone through the conservatory and upstairs—just as I did." He turned on the porter. "Is there anybody upstairs now? Any attendant, I mean?"

"No, sir. Not except me. It's ha' past eleven, you know. Ha' past eleven."

"Have you seen any outsider hanging about here?"

"No, sir. Not except you. I been up in my cubby-hole, having forty winks. Speaking personally," added the porter, with dark significance, "I don't 'old with games. Not speaking personally."

"Games! Look there!"

He walked along the edge of the pool and pointed. The greenish water still ran in waves, blurring vision. But it was so clear that they could all discern the object lying at the bottom of the pool a few inches away from the wall, and towards the middle of the long side. It was a shiny metal object, shaped like a knife with a broad hilt. There seemed to be some lettering along it.

As she recalled, Jane's hand flew inside her robe and touched her left arm just below the shoulder. While the two others peered at the knife, she pulled away an edge of the robe to look. There was a very slight puncture, hardly breaking the skin, which had begun to bleed a drop or two. The arm felt sore, but she found no other injury.

Fred whirled round.

"Are you hurt?"

"No. Not a scratch. Please! Don't bother!"

"Nor I shouldn't neither," declared the porter. "As the young lady says. Do you know what that thing is? It's a paperknife."

"A what?"

"A paperknife. It's blunt. It couldn't hurt nobody, no matter how hard you tried. It comes from the lounge upstairs, or maybe from somewhere else. Ah, sir, you don't believe me? You're still undressed. Hop in and get it and see."

Fred did so. When he emerged with it, the porter radiated satisfaction. Down the blade were carved the words, inlaid with gilt, *Esplanade Hotel, Tawnish*. The sides of the knife were partly rounded and the point so blunt that it was obvious no great harm could be done with it in any case. The porter wiped it off on his shirt and put it away in his pocket.

"Speaking personally," he said, "I don't 'old with games. Not speaking personally."

"All right. We want our clothes."

"I don't know as I ought to get 'em for you, sir."

"All right again. Then I'll walk out of this damn place in my bathing-suit, and tell the first policeman who stops me that the Esplanade Hotel wouldn't give up my trousers." He was growing light-headed with anger. "I had also thought that you might be persuaded to accept a pound note for your trouble, but if that's how you feel about it—"

"Sh-h! Fred! It's all right! He'll unlock the dressing-rooms for us. Won't you?"

"I didn't say I *wouldn't*, miss. I just said you hadn't ought to 'a' been down here, after it was all locked up. That's not really right; now is it? But if you'll come this way, I *will* stretch a point and open up for you."

As he was unlocking the doors, another idea struck Fred Barlow.

"Just a minute," Fred requested; and made off again.

Though the porter uttered a howl of despair behind him, he kept on his way. A broad flight of stairs with padded carpet led up past several landings to the main floor. Fred took the steps three at a time. This attack on Jane, which could not have been meant seriously to injure her, worried him nearly as much as though it had.

It was meaningless. It did not fit in. A threat? Or a wanton, childish gesture, meant to frighten? It looked very much like the latter. In which case—

The main hall upstairs was large, breezy, and dark. Its marble floor felt considerably chillier than the one downstairs, and Fred did not linger. At the back, big glass doors opened into the main lounge, where a few late lights glowed. The lounge was full of palms, and in the middle a fountain tinkled somnolently.

In an easychair, equally somnolent, sat Dr. Gideon Fell.

His eyeglasses drooped. His pipe had slipped out of his mouth, but was prevented from falling by mountainous ridges of waistcoat. Mysterious internal wheezings blew through his nostrils, making him seem to jump from time to time. But at Fred's approach he started, grunted, and opened one eye.

"Have you been here long?" Fred asked.

"Eh? Oh! For some time, yes."

"Asleep?"

"To be candid, I was plotting devilment." He fumbled

for his eyeglasses, and blinked through them. "Wow!" he observed. "If you don't mind my saying so, you resemble the sandalled friar of legend, though somewhat less holy and considerably wetter. What in blazes have you been up to?"

Fred disregarded this.

"Have you seen anybody come through this lounge—from the back to the front—in the last few minutes?"

"Come to think of it, I saw *you* come stalking through about ten minutes ago. But I didn't believe it. I thought I must have dreamed you."

"No, I mean after that. Going in the same direction, though. Did you?"

"Nobody but Mr. Appleby."

"Appleby!"

"Our friend the solicitor. Presumably on his way to bed. I wasn't in a mood to have a word with him, though I understand he's interviewed Graham tonight." The doctor paused. "Still, you notice all these palms. I shouldn't necessarily have seen anyone unless he walked down the main aisle. What is it?"

Fred told him.

The drowsiness of sleep or concentration was struck off Dr. Fell's face.

"I don't like it," he growled.

"No."

"It doesn't fit."

"Exactly what I was thinking."

Fred was about to turn away and give it up as a bad job. All the hotel staff were in bed except the night-porter, who had been drowsing in a dark foyer; any person, provided he kept behind the palms, could have slipped through and out without attracting the attention of Dr. Fell.

Yet he hesitated. Something about the doctor's manner tapped out a message of warning to his brain. Dr. Fell's fists were clenched, his eye evasive; he seemed uncertain, and, at the same time, heavily embarrassed. Many possibilities, none pleasant, occurred to Fred.

"I suppose," he said over his shoulder, "you and Inspector Graham have been having a busy time?"

"Oh, yes. Very busy."

"Anything new?"

"Some new evidence. We had, in a sense, to dig for it. We have been over the place." As though coming to a decision, Dr. Fell settled back in his chair. "By the way," he added, "we have also had a little talk with one George Herbert Diehl, better known hereabouts as Black Jeff."

The fountain sang whisperingly. Fred contemplated the floor, rocking back and forth on his heels. He did not raise his eyes.

"Oh? Was he hurt, then? Badly?"

"Hurt?" said Dr. Fell. "He was not hurt at all. But it would be interesting, Mr. Barlow, to hear why you thought he was."

Fred laughed. "I didn't say he was. If you remember what I told Graham, I said I was afraid he might be, when I saw him lying in the road. But I'm glad to hear it. Not hurt at all, then?"

"A healthier, dirtier specimen," replied Dr. Fell, "I have seldom seen. We found him pigging it in one of those model houses up Lovers' Lane, which Graham tells me is his usual hangout. He was recovering from his spree, and eating tinned sardines for afternoon breakfast. Here! Steady on! What's the matter?"

"Nothing. Go on."

Dr. Fell eyed him.

"If the matter is of any interest to you, sir (though I can't imagine why it should be), he says he has no recollection of anything that happened between Friday night and Sunday morning. Which is a pity. If he had been in the vicinity of Lovers' Lane on Saturday night—near a certain telephone-box, say—he might be in a position to verify something interesting."

"Is that so? What?"

This time it was Dr. Fell who ignored a question.

"His whiskers really are remarkable. I also like his butcher's coat and his bandana handkerchief. But as a witness—no. No, I think not."

"Well, I'll be getting on, Doctor. Goodnight."

"Yes, you look a bit done in. Take an aspirin and some whisky, and go to bed. If you are anywhere near Horace Ireton's bungalow tomorrow after lunch, it might pay you to look in. Inspector Graham has some ideas under his hat which may surprise everybody. I pass the tip on gratis."

The tinkle of the fountain went on interminably. Fred found it difficult to move away. It was like one of those conversations over the telephone in which neither party knows quite what to say to end it. Dr. Fell appeared to be feeling much the same trouble. Fred said something of a hearty nature, and broke the strands by starting for the door. Even then he had only taken five steps before the doctor's big voice stopped him.

"Mr. Barlow!"

"Yes?"

"Will you think me ill-mannered," said Dr. Fell, screwing up a face which was tolerably red and distressed already, "if I say that I should like to offer you my condolences beforehand?"

Fred stared at him.

"Condolences? What exactly do you mean?"

"Just that. I anticipate. But I should like to offer you my condolences beforehand. Goodnight."

CHAPTER XVII

THE ECKMANN ESTATE AND HOUSING COMPANY, now defunct, had once cherished great plans for the rural road which they had re-named Wellington Avenue but which was still locally known as Lovers' Lane.

It was to be a centre, a focus. From it were to spring out those fine developments of moderate-priced houses (£650 to £950) whose streets were already laid out on charts in the office of the company as Cromwell Avenue, Marlborough Avenue, Wolfe Avenue, and so on.

These streets were still nettles and red clay. But Lovers' Lane, the only proper road which joined the main road between Tawnish and Horseshoe Bay, had been surfaced with concrete. A telephone-box was set up. It stood some twenty yards beyond the entrance, where the banks which closed in Lovers' Lane broadened and flattened to pleasant open country. Here the concrete stopped, shredding away into clay and scattered gravel. Here, in a cleared space, a model detached house stood on one side of the road, and two model semi-detached houses stood on the other.

These houses were crumbling and darkening. They had once been red brick and white stucco. But they could not be bought or rented even if anyone had wanted them: the legal title remained in dispute, complicated by the position of one of the directors, who was doing a stretch on Dartmoor. Children revelled in them; amorous couples had once or twice caused a scandal there; the wind loosened their shutters and rats gnawed at their roots.

Early in the afternoon of Monday, April twenty-ninth—a bright day, with patches of overcast sky—Constance Ireton turned off the main road and walked up Lovers' Lane.

She was bareheaded, though she wore a fur-trimmed coat over her dark frock. Her fair hair was dressed far from elaborately, and she had very little makeup. This may have been what made her appear older. It was only last Thursday since she had talked with Tony Morell in the little garden behind the sessions-house, on the afternoon that John Edward Lypiatt was sentenced to die. Yet she seemed older.

Constance did not seem, either, to have much purpose, or direction about her. She scuffed at the road with her shoe. She had the air of one who is wandering under compulsion. She frowned at the telephone-box, but she did not stop there.

The concrete of the road was cracked; it was always bad concrete. After hesitating, she wandered on up towards the model houses. She had almost reached them when she stopped again—suddenly.

"Hello!" said a voice in which surprise was mingled with relief.

Outside one of the semi-detached houses on the right stood a familiar motor car. It was a Cadillac with red upholstery. Its cleanness stood out in contrast to the crumbling house behind. She recognized the car even before she recognized the voice. Jane Tennant, pulling on gloves, came down the two steps of the house.

"Connie!"

Constance made a movement as though to turn and run. But the other hurried across a patch of what was once supposed to have been front garden, and intercepted her.

"Connie, where on earth have you been? We've been worried to death about you."

"I came over and stayed at Daddy's bungalow. I took the bus. Why shouldn't I?"

"But couldn't you have 'phoned us and told us where you were?"

"No, thanks," answered Constance, rather sullenly. "I've had enough trouble over telephones as it is."

Jane seemed a little taken aback. Though she was again muffled in country tweeds, the vividness and softness of her face redeemed its lack of beauty. Constance did not look at her; but she seemed aware of this.

"They all asked me to say goodbye to you for them," Jane went on. "They were terribly sorry not to have seen you before they went—"

"They're not *gone*? Everybody?"

"Yes; they left this morning. It's Monday, you know. Hugo Raikes in particular asked me to remind you of something or other; he didn't specify what."

Constance studied the ground and smiled, thoughtfully.

"Yes, Hugo's rather nice, isn't he? He knows how to *enjoy* himself. Other people don't. Except for—"

"Except for what?"

"Nothing."

"He's got a terrible hangover this morning," said Jane practically. "And a bad welt on his forehead from trying fancy dives off the high board."

"Oh? How did the swimming-party go?"

"Marvellously!"

"You seem to have enjoyed yourself."

"I did."

"Oh. And how's that dreadful slut in the red bathing-suit, who hangs about him so much?"

"Laura Cornish?—Connie," said Jane quietly, "how do you know she wore a red bathing-suit?"

The sun was dead pale and very brilliant, only different from the colour of the sky by its blaze. It was veiled and then revealed again by moving, dull-grey clouds. Here on higher ground the wind blew cold. A stray fowl scuttled in the middle of what should have been Wellington Avenue, rasping scattered gravel.

"Connie, I want to talk to you. Let's go across the way, shall we?"

"All right. Though I don't see why you should want to talk to *me*."

The detached house across the road, presumably once the pride of Messrs Eckmann & Co., had window-frames painted green against red brick and once-white stucco. All these window panes were grimy; some were broken. The front door, set under a brick arch, drooped off its frame. There was a lean-to garage built out at the side.

"Where are we going?" Constance demanded.

"Here. I'll show you."

"And what are you doing here anyway, Jane Tennant? What are you *doing* up here?"

"I was trying to find a tramp called Black Jeff. His stuff's in the other house; but he's not here. What are *you* doing here, if it comes to that?"

"Because I hadn't anywhere else to go, really," returned Constance. "They chased me out of the house. They're all down at the bungalow now, Daddy and Fred Barlow and Dr. Fell and Inspector Graham, going on like mad. The little girl must go out and play while they talk about serious business." She paused as Jane pushed open the sagging door. "In there?"

"In there."

The little hall still had a small Venetian lantern hanging from the roof. They went through into a kitchen, dim with dust. Its walls, above the tiling, were scrawled with initials and messages written in pencil. An empty beer-bottle stood on top of the electric refrigerator. Jane closed the door.

"Nobody can hear us now," she said. She put her handbag on the refrigerator-top. She clenched her hands against the sharp pain of uncertainty which was hurting her. "Connie," she added quietly, "it was really you who went for me last night at the swimming-pool, wasn't it?"

"Yes," answered Constance, after a pause.

Nothing more than that.

"But why? In heaven's name, why? Why do you dislike me so much?"

"I don't dislike you. I envy you."

"Envy?"

Constance had backed against the sink, holding to its edge with her hands on either side of her. To judge by her tone, she felt little emotion of any kind. Her eyes were large, brown, and quick-moving; they regarded Jane with real curiosity.

"You haven't got any parents, have you?"

"Not living, no."

"And you've got lots and lots of money, all your own?"

"Some."

"Nobody," said Constance, "to say yes or no to you. And you're older than I am, so if you do what you like nobody thinks it's odd of you—as they always do with me. That's it: you're older than I am. I wish I were thirty-five. I might be old and wrinkled…"

"Connie, my dear, good *fool*—!"

"But at least nobody would be surprised at what I did. You do as you like. If you want to go to Cannes, or St Moritz, you can go. If you want to entertain people, you entertain people. But do you enjoy it? No. Not you. You didn't enjoy having those people in your house a minute, did you?"

Her voice trailed off to a whisper. It was little above a whisper when she spoke again.

"Jane, I'm horribly, horribly sorry. I swear to God I didn't mean to hurt you!"

Before Jane could intervene, she hurried on.

"I was jealous of you and Fred, in a way. I followed Fred. I wanted to frighten you. Just frighten you, and make you as upset and unhappy as I'd been feeling. I followed Fred because I knew you'd invite him to that party even before you did. I got that paperknife out of the lounge. I wore gloves because that's what they always do in the detective stories. Are you furious with me?"

"Oh, Connie, don't you see it doesn't *matter*?"

Constance's mind caught only one part of this.

"You're not furious with me?" she asked incredulously.

"No, of course not."

"I don't believe it."

"Connie, my dear, listen. That isn't the important part. Did you—well, did you happen to overhear what Fred and I were saying to each other?"

"Yes, I did. And saw you." Now Constance spoke with the utmost quiet, the quiet of conviction. "I think it was revolting. I'm not being catty or nasty now, Jane; really I'm not. But I do think so. I should never let—"

Jane's hands relaxed at her sides. She drew a deep breath. From the grey eyes uncertainty slowly cleared away, as did even the baffled expression.

"Connie," she said, "you're a child. You really are a child. I never quite realized that until now."

"Don't you say that to me too!"

"Wait. Connie, do you love Fred Barlow?"

"No, of course not. I like him, naturally; but he's no more exciting than a brother would be."

"Were you ever really in love with Tony Morell?"

"Yes. Terribly! But do you know"—Constance looked down and scuffed at the floor, and wrinkled up her forehead—"do you know, now he's gone and can't come back, I don't seem to *miss* him so much. I was always a bit uncomfortable when he was about. You mustn't tell that to anybody, Jane, but I was. I think Hugo Raikes is much nicer. Not that I could ever feel for Hugo what I felt for Tony, of course; my life's ruined and I'll just have to make the best of it; but still I do feel that Hugo is ever so nice to go to parties with."

Jane began to laugh. She stopped immediately, for Constance imagined that she was laughing at these sentiments rather than at all the implications behind them. Her eyes strayed past Constance, out of the grimy window over the sink, at the sun brightening and darkening over the half-wintry landscape. It was bitter laughter; it ended with something like a sob.

She fought this away.

"Connie, have the police found you yet?"

"No."

"You know they're looking for you?"

"Yes. Daddy hid me away at the bungalow last night, when they asked after me. I never thought he could be so human, Jane. He said he wanted time to think."

"You've heard why they're looking for you?"

"Y-yes."

Jane's voice was fierce with sincerity. "I want you to believe that I'm your friend. It's true, whether you believe it or not. Your father's in great danger, Connie. I'm not trying to scare you: I only want you to realize something."

"I'd do anything," said Constance simply, "to get him out of it."

"On Saturday night, at twenty minutes past eight, you tried to put a call through to my house from that telephone-box down the lane. You were trying to get in touch with me. Connie, what did you want to tell me?"

Taking her hands off the edge of the sink, Constance stood

up straight. She seemed surprised to find that her fingers were cramped and stiff where she had gripped. She drew her coat closely round her.

"This place is dreadful," she remarked, with the composure of a mannequin exhibiting clothes, and with something of the same slow deliberation. "I'm sure I don't know why you want to stay here talking. And not getting anywhere either. I'm going." Her voice grew apprehensive. "You won't try to stop me?"

"No, I won't try to stop you. But, Connie…"

She received no reply. Constance walked past her, opened the door, and went out through the hall into the ghost of a street.

After a hesitation, Jane picked up her handbag and followed. She found Constance standing at the top of the gravelly road, as though elaborately unconscious of anybody near her, and only wondering where to go next in her stroll.

From the top of this slight rise a path wandered across the fields. It descended past scrub trees emaciated by the sea wind. Three hundred yards away, partly hidden by trees, they could see the edge of Mr. Justice Ireton's bungalow. The sea was visible from here, too: a dim, bluish haze stung with light-points when the sun emerged.

Jane asked her question.

"Connie, did your father kill Tony Morell?"

Constance spoke breathlessly. "No! No! No! And if it's the last words I ever say—"

She stiffened. So did Jane. They both turned, determined figures on that windy hillside, and looked across the fields towards the judge's bungalow. The same question was in both their minds. From that direction, borne by the wind, faintly muffled but crashing with ugly distinctness, they heard a shot fired.

CHAPTER XVIII

SOME TWENTY MINUTES OR HALF AN HOUR BEFORE THAT event occurred, Mr. Justice Ireton watched his daughter go out by the front gate. He watched her stroll off aimlessly up the road. Then he turned back to his three guests.

"And to what, gentlemen," he inquired, "do I owe the honour of this unexpected visit?"

He was this morning in town clothes. His dark coat, striped trousers, wing collar, and grey tie were all immaculate. They gave him—the impression is hard to describe—a fussy appearance which was not lessened by his snappish manner over a cold, polite patience.

Dr. Fell sat on the sofa, Frederick Barlow on the arm of the sofa. Inspector Graham occupied one of the easychairs, and had his notebook on the chess table.

"I still think, sir," Graham said slowly, "it'd have been better to let Miss Ireton stay, like she wanted to. We shall only have to fetch her back, I'm afraid."

Even though this might be only his usual form of attack, Graham's face was very grave.

"She will be within call, if you want her. Meanwhile, I am still waiting. To what do I owe the honour of this unexpected visit?"

"Well, sir," said Graham, hunching up his shoulders rather nervously, and clearing his throat once or twice before he resumed, "it's like this. Early this morning I had a conference with my Super and the Chief Constable. We've been all over this business. It's not a thing we like. So they can't see, any more than I can, that much good would be served by waiting any longer."

"Waiting any longer, for what?"

"To make an arrest," replied Graham.

Mr. Justice Ireton closed and latched the French window, which darkened the room still more.

He returned to his usual chair, sat down, and crossed his legs.

"Go on," he said.

Graham brooded.

"You see, sir, it's like this. I got off on the wrong foot in this business. I admit that. I was on the right track, maybe, but I didn't notice a lot of things that were right under my nose all the time, until Dr. Fell showed 'em to me."

The upholstery of the gaudy chair was of some roughish material. They heard Mr. Justice Ireton's fingernails scratching at the arms of it, as he opened and shut his hands.

"Indeed." He glanced at Dr. Fell. "So it is to your—ah—lucubrations, sir, that we are indebted for what we think we have learned now?"

"No!" said Dr. Fell firmly. His big voice roared out of the

gloom, and he lowered it. "I was only able to show, by good luck, *how* this murder was committed. For the rest, I take no responsibility."

"How the murder was committed?" repeated Mr. Justice Ireton, in frank wonder. "Was there ever any doubt as to how it was committed?"

"My good sir," said Dr. Fell, "there was never any doubt in my mind on any point except that. With your permission, we propose to explain it to you."

"I am forgetting my hospitality," remarked the judge, after a pause. "Will you take some refreshment, gentlemen?"

"Not for me, thanks," said Graham.

"No, I thank you," said Dr. Fell.

"I'll have a spot, sir," said Fred Barlow.

Mr. Justice Ireton went to the sideboard. He poured a whisky-and-soda for his guest, and for himself a thimbleful of brandy from an old, squat bottle. He handled the big goblet-glass as tenderly as though it contained liquid gold: as, in a sense, it did. After clipping and lighting a cigar, he returned to his chair. He sat warming the glass, swirling its contents round gently, while the sun flashed and darkened outside the windows, and he regarded his guests with composure.

"I am waiting."

"The difficulty in this affair," said Dr. Fell, "was that from the start nobody seems to have noticed one very important thing. We saw it. It thrust itself upon our attention. Yet for some curious reason nobody seems to have realized what it meant. I refer to the following fact. *Round the bullet-wound in Morell's head there were no powder-marks.*"

Mr. Justice Ireton frowned.

"Well?"

"I repeat," insisted Dr. Fell. "There was no sign of powder-singeing. Now, I hardly have to tell you what that means. It means that the revolver was not held directly against Morell's head when the shot was fired. On the contrary, the weapon must have been held at least five or six inches away, and probably a much greater distance. We have no means of telling."

He drew in his breath in a long sniff.

"Now observe what follows. We know that the shot was fired on the instant that Morell uttered his final word—'Help!'—to the telephone operator. But how does anybody speak to a telephone? He speaks with his lips almost against the mouthpiece. His head shields the telephone, his lips shield the mouthpiece.

"This bullet which killed Morell was fired from behind. It entered the back of the head behind the right ear. The weapon was held some distance away.

"Then can you blame me for being astounded when I find that inside the edge of the mouthpiece—*inside*—there are distinct powder-marks? Can you blame me for being astounded when I see that a shot fired from some distance back, with Morell's head intervening between it and the telephone, not only left powder-marks in the mouthpiece but had an explosion strong enough to crack the sounding-drum inside?"

Dr. Fell sat up.

He said quietly:

"I say to you, gentlemen, that this is impossible. I say to you that, when this particular shot was fired at half past eight, no head could have intervened. I say to you that the revolver must have been held within an inch of that mouthpiece, pointing sideways past it, so that a few powder-grains stung the inside. I say to you, therefore, that the shot heard at half past eight could not have been the shot which killed Anthony Morell."

Dr. Fell paused. He ran his hands through his grey-streaked mop of hair, with an expression of acute discomfort and even perplexity.

"That's clear, isn't it?" he inquired, glancing from one to the other. "You were all so disdainful when I expressed surprise about the telephone that I can't help asking."

Mr. Justice Ireton swallowed brandy.

"The explanation," he conceded, "appears probable. Then it follows—?"

Dr. Fell made a gesture.

"Why," he said, "it follows that Morell did not whisper those words, 'The Dunes. Ireton's bungalow. Help!' It follows that some other person did whisper them, and then deliberately fired a shot almost into the mouthpiece of the telephone, so that there should be no doubt in the operator's mind of what had happened. It follows that the whole thing was a fake and a plant."

"Designed?"

"Designed by the murderer," said Dr. Fell, "to show that Morell had died at that particular time and in that particular place."

Inspector Graham fiddled with his notebook. Fred Barlow finished his whisky-and-soda. And Dr. Fell went on.

"So much became clear after an examination of this room on Saturday night. Two shots, then, were fired. The first shot presumably killed Morell, who died at some time previous to eight-thirty. The second was fired in here. But only one spent cartridge-case was found in the revolver later. Consequently, the murderer must have slipped another bullet into the magazine for the second shot, to make us believe only one had been fired.

"Now this raised two interesting points. First, where did this extra bullet come from? Did the murderer carry a spare for that purpose? Or a blank cartridge, perhaps? Or—"

Dr. Fell broke off. With an air of apology he pointed at the chess table.

"On Saturday night, musing densely over these points, I wandered up against that chess table. I found the chess pieces and began to mess about with them. I was throwing up and catching one of them, with utter absence of mind, when a great light blazed over these feeble wits of mine. For I remembered a certain habit of Morell's; and I remembered his pocket-piece."

Mr. Justice Ireton seemed nonplussed for the first time. When he took the cigar out of his mouth, Inspector Graham could see teeth-marks on the end of it. But the judge's voice remained even.

"His pocket-piece? I do not understand."

"His lucky-piece," explained Dr. Fell. "His mascot. It was a bullet, a ·32 calibre revolver bullet. His habit was to toss it up and catch it. Those who knew him, including Miss Tennant, will tell you that his lucky-piece was never, never anywhere or at any time, off his person. Yet, I remembered, PC Weems had just finished reading out a list of all the articles found in Morell's pockets; and this bullet was *not* among them."

"Ah," murmured Mr. Justice Ireton, finishing his brandy.

"But that led to the second point. If this bullet, or any bullet for that matter, had been fired as the second shot, then where in blazes had it gone?"

He paused, and looked at them ferociously.

"It was not in the room. Inspector Graham assured me of that. He assured me that every crack and crevice of this room had been searched, without the police finding anything, anything at all, except what we knew. The more I pestered him about this, as he was driving me to the hotel on Saturday night, the more emphatic he became. Yet the bullet could not have got out. Therefore, logically, it must be here."

The judge smiled.

"Now that," he pointed out, "is not logic; it is reluctance to discard a cherished theory. For the bullet is not here."

"Oh, yes it is," said Dr. Fell.

The windows had darkened again, so that they could see little more than a wheezing shape as Dr. Fell hoisted himself to his feet.

"With your permission, Inspector Graham will now show you exactly what the murderer did. I am not spry enough to execute all the movements myself."

But for once the spectators were not looking at him. They were looking at Inspector Graham. With entire gravity, and a kind of dogged purposefulness, Graham had taken out of his pocket what closer inspection enabled Fred Barlow to identify as a packet of Toni-Sweet Chewing-Gum. Graham removed the wrapper from a stick of the gum, and put it into his mouth.

The judge surveyed him, but did not say anything. Mr.

Justice Ireton's expression was the same as that with which he had once regarded Tony Morell.

"Of course," Dr. Fell resumed, "I should have tumbled to it much sooner. There were three almost certain indications of the direction we ought to look.

"I mean first of all the telephone, which had already bothered me so much. It bothered me at the start, because, as I told you then, I didn't see how that 'phone could have got so smashed about merely by being knocked off the desk. It looked almost as though someone had flung it violently down. Or else—held it up in the air at some height, and dropped it on the floor.

"Then there was that little cushion on the seat of the swivel desk chair. I examined it, and it was grimy. Grimy in an otherwise neat house. Inspector Graham, I am told, had at one time earlier in the evening picked it up and slapped at it to clear away traces of dirt. Almost as though somebody with damp boots had stood on that cushion.

"Finally, there was this."

Dr. Fell lumbered across to the desk; where, after standing towards one side so that they could see, he pulled the chain of the little desk lamp. Again the brilliant little circle of light stretched out across the desk and the floor, as in Graham's demonstration the day before.

"Mr. Justice Ireton," Dr. Fell went on, "tells us that when *he* left this room to go to the kitchen at twenty minutes past eight, only this lamp was burning. Between then and half past eight somebody switched on the central chandelier. Why? Well, you observe that the desk lamp has an immovable metal shade. It lights only the desk and the floor. It does not light the upper part of the room.

"Taken in connection with the indications that (*a*) somebody stood up on the cushion of the desk chair, and (*b*) somebody held up the telephone at some height before dropping it, there is only one place for us to look. There is, indeed, only one thing we can look for."

Dr. Fell turned round and walked to the central light-switch beside the door to the hall. The blaze of the central chandelier, as he pressed the switch, blinded them all until their eyes grew accustomed to it.

"There it is," said Dr. Fell.

Grotesquely, the stuffed moose's head looked back at them from the wall up over the desk. It was old and tawdry and moth-eaten. It went with the bilious blue-flowered wallpaper and the woven sofa-cushions.

Mr. Justice Ireton's voice sounded thin and harsh, off-guard now and half hysterical with surprise.

"You are saying—?"

"Show them, Graham," suggested Dr. Fell.

Inspector Graham got up. From his hip-pocket he took the Ives-Grant ·32 revolver, and tested it to make sure the cylinder would turn to the movement of the hammer.

Walking over to the desk, he set the swivel-chair some two feet out in front of it, a little to the left of the moose's head. He shifted the revolver to his left hand. He took the telephone receiver off its hook. Wrapping a handkerchief round his right hand, he picked up both 'phone and receiver in the same hand. With these in his right hand and the revolver in his left, he climbed up on the chair. It creaked and cracked sharply as he balanced himself.

His own eyes were now almost on a level with the glass

ones. He pointed the revolver at the indentation or cavity formed by the right nostril of the grotesque stuffed head. Drawing the telephone-cord to its full length, he held the 'phone close to the revolver. He bent close to both.

Then he spoke softly but clearly.

"*The Dunes. Ireton's cottage. Help!*" said Graham. He jerked back his head—and fired.

The crash of the shot blasted in that enclosed place. What happened afterwards was too quick for Fred Barlow's eye to follow except in retrospect.

The telephone, released, clattered and banged down on the floor. The handkerchief fluttered after it. Graham's right hand made a short movement before it darted to the left nostril of the head, into which he had fired a bullet. Just before it reached there, something curious seemed to be happening to the carpet on the floor beside Graham's chair.

Pale red sand began to materialize there, as though an invisible hour-glass had been tilted up. It flickered in the air. It dusted into a tiny pyramid, scattering a little, just before Graham's big thumb pressed hard into the nostril of the stuffed head.

"Got it!" breathed the Inspector. The chair creaked agonizedly under him; he swayed, and almost fell. "Chewing-gum is good for *something*, anyhow. It plugs up a ·32 bullet-hole as neat as putty. And, with the colour of it, you'll never be able to tell it from the plaster-of-paris inside when it hardens."

There was a silence.

"Yes," sighed Dr. Fell, as the others looked at him, "that's the whole story. But I never guessed it until I sat on the balcony of my hotel-room yesterday and watched three men filling sandbags across the street, while somebody informed me that the late owner of this bungalow was a Canadian.

"It's the custom of many taxidermists in Canada and the United States to stuff largish heads, under the external hard composition and layers of tallow-rag, with fine sand. I should have realized when I saw the head. We don't have moose running about in England, you know. The point is that that thing is a natural sandbag: nothing more or less. And a sandbag will easily stop a light-calibre revolver bullet."

He returned to the sofa and sat down.

Inspector Graham jumped down from the chair, dusting a few grains of sand from his tunic. His weight made the floor shake.

He put the revolver down on the desk.

"Not much doubt about that," Graham observed grimly. "In fact, it buried two. The one fired on Saturday night is on the other side of the same head."

"Most ingenious," observed Mr. Justice Ireton.

He seemed to be trying to clear his throat, a delicate operation, which necessitated moving his neck. Yet still not a muscle moved in his face.

"You say," resumed the judge thoughtfully, "that 'somebody' did that?"

"Yes, sir. The murderer."

"Indeed. Then how do you suggest that I—"

Graham stared at him.

"*You?*" he exploded. "Lord God, sir, we don't think for a minute *you* did it! In fact, we know you didn't."

Outside the windows, running footsteps pounded up the lawn. One of the windows was flung open. Constance Ireton, followed by Jane Tennant, ran into the room and stopped short. Yet so great was the emotional tensity of the other four persons, or perhaps only three of them, that the entrance of the girls went unnoticed until Constance spoke.

"We heard a shot," she said in a thin high voice. "We heard a *shot*."

Her father craned round. He seemed to wake up to exasperation as he saw her. He waved his hand, as though he were shooing away a servant.

"Constance," he said coldly, "be good enough not to intrude at a moment like this. Your presence is inconvenient. Go away, please; and take this"—he put on his spectacles—"this young lady with you."

But Graham intervened.

"No," the Inspector said, with a sort of comfortable grimness.

"You stay where you are, miss. I've got an idea, just a bit of an idea, we shall be wanting you before many minutes."

Then he resumed his earnest speech to the judge.

"You see, sir, it's not likely that you, of all people, would try any such funny business: in your own house, putting the rope around your own neck. No, sir. It's somebody else who did that for you. Now, this is all *fact*. We can prove it. There's other facts too. As soon as we found 'em—well, that settled it. Ask Dr. Fell.

"Every word of the story you told us, crazy as it sounded, was true. That's clear now. The murderer dumped Morell's dead body in here while you were out in the kitchen. The murderer turned on the lights, set the stage, and fired the fake bullet. Then the murderer pushed Morell's body on the red sand and nipped out of here."

"We heard a *shot*," Constance insisted, in the same piercing voice.

Graham turned round.

"Yes, miss, you did," he agreed; and proceeded to give the two newcomers a leisurely account of everything that had happened.

Neither Constance nor Jane commented. The former was very white, the latter quiet but with eyes of intense watchfulness. The brilliant chandelier lights picked out every movement of their faces.

"So Tony wasn't shot," Constance breathed, and then paused, "here."

"No, miss."

"And he wasn't shot—at half past eight."

"No, miss. Some minutes before then. Not very long before; not long enough so any doctor could ever tell the difference of a few minutes in the time."

"And he couldn't have been killed by—Daddy."

"No, miss. I was coming to that. There's only one person, only one, who could have killed him. There's only one person who had any reason to try to change the time and place of the killing. There's only one person who *had* to make us believe Mr. Morell was shot here at half past eight, instead of in another place at another time: or else he was dished for good. We've now got the evidence against that person. I'll show it to you in half a second."

Graham paused. He drew himself up. His strawberry rash was violent, and he took a breath like one who intends to dive underwater. Then he walked across the room, and put his hand on a certain person's shoulder.

He said:

"*Frederick Barlow, I must ask you to accompany me to Tawnish police-station. There you will be formally charged with the murder of Anthony Morell, and placed in custody to appear before the magistrates in Exeter a week from today.*"

CHAPTER XIX

AFTERWARDS, LONG AFTERWARDS, DR. GIDEON FELL tried to recall the expressions on the faces of those present when they heard this accusation.

It was difficult. He remembered the colours of clothes, the positions in which people were standing or sitting, even the fall of shadows, better than that other clay-like blur. He remembered that Constance put a hand to her mouth. He remembered that Mr. Justice Ireton merely nodded, as though dispassionately waiting to hear. But everything else was swallowed up in the impression of anguish, of deadly fear and anguish, which flowed from Jane Tennant and held her dumb.

Fred Barlow, on the arm of the sofa, had his head turned sideways to Dr. Fell. He wore a brown-and-black sports coat, and his hair was unruly. Dr. Fell could see the profile, as clean as the profile on a coin, and the muscles tightening down the side of the jaw.

"So you think *I* did it?" he remarked, without apparent surprise.

"Naturally, sir. I'm sorry."

"Inspector," said Fred, "where was Morell really killed? In your opinion?"

"Opposite the entrance to Lovers' Lane. On the patch of sand and scrub-grass across the main road from there."

"And at what time was he killed? Again in your opinion?"

"In my opinion—which I can prove, mind you—between fifteen and twenty minutes past eight o'clock."

Fred's fingers tapped, and tapped again, on his knee.

"Before I go along to the police-station," he said in a hard, level voice, "I'd like to ask a favour. You say you have definite, conclusive evidence against me. Will you tell me what that evidence is, here and now? I know you're not obliged to do it. I know it's irregular to do it. But will you do me that courtesy?"

"Yes, I will," retorted Inspector Graham.

He went back to the desk. From under it, invisible until now, he fished out a small brown leather suitcase. This he brought back and put on the chess table. His strawberry rash was up. He addressed himself to the judge.

"Here's how it is, sir. In Tawnish we've got a doctor, a local GP by the name of Dr. Hulworthy Fellows. Don't mix him up with Dr. Fell; though it's odd, now you come to think of it, that those two should have been a kind of nemesis for Mr. Fred Barlow."

"Spare us these comments," said the judge. "State your evidence. I will tell you if there is anything in it."

"It's a pleasure, sir," Graham said through his teeth. "All right. On Saturday night, after dark, Dr. Fellows was summoned out to an urgent case at Cooldown, on the other side of Horseshoe Bay. Just as he was driving along the main road—towards Horseshoe Bay—and when he'd nearly got as far as Lovers' Lane, the headlights of his car picked up a man who was lying on the sand at the side of the road. This man was lying with his back to the doctor. There wasn't a lot of light. All Dr. Fellows could see was that he seemed to be a squarish sort of chap, with very black hair, in a greyish kind of coat. Over him stood Mr. Barlow, looking (this is what the doctor says) 'as though he'd done a murder.'"

Inspector Graham paused.

"Now, then. The doctor called out and said, 'What's wrong?' Thinking there'd been an accident, you see, and stopping. Mr. Barlow said, 'It's Black Jeff; he's drunk again.' Not a word about an accident, according to the doctor. So that was enough for Dr. Fellows. He said, 'Oh roll him down the beach! the tide'll sober him up,' and drove on."

Again Graham paused.

"He didn't get out to investigate. But, unfortunately, he'd seen Mr. Barlow with the body of the man Mr. Barlow had just killed. So something had to be done about it."

Mr. Justice Ireton considered this.

"You are going to suggest," he said, "that the supposed figure of Black Jeff the tramp was really the dead body of Mr. Morell?"

"No, sir," returned Graham, undoing the catches of the suitcase with a click. "I'm not going to suggest it. I'm going to *prove* it."

He opened the suitcase.

"And what time was this?" Fred asked, still without moving.

"The doctor"—Graham lowered the lid of the suitcase again—"the doctor says he looked at his dashboard clock, to see how much time he'd got to make Cooldown. He says the time was twenty-one or twenty-two minutes past eight, more or less. Where were you then, Mr. Barlow?"

"Precisely where the doctor says I was...so you maintain."

"Ah? You admit that, sir?"

"No," interposed the judge. "I cannot allow this. Inspector, this gentleman is not yet under arrest. You have not cautioned him. Such a question, therefore, is improper and illegal; and any attempt you make to use it as evidence will be attended with most unpleasant results."

"Just as you like, sir," snapped Graham. "Maybe you'd rather see this, then."

From the suitcase he took a small cardboard box, whose lid he removed to show a tiny brass cylinder.

"We've got here," he went on, "what I'll call Exhibit A. Exploded cartridge-case of Ives-Grant ·32 revolver bullet. Got a distinctive hammer-mark, this one has. Matches the hammer-mark of exploded cartridge-case now in the magazine of that revolver over there. Both were fired from that gun, our ballistics man says. In other words, all that's left of the bullet that killed Mr. Morell." Graham added: "Found in the sand not very many feet away from where Mr. Barlow admits he was standing."

Graham replaced the lid on the box, and returned it to the suitcase. He now took out a flattish tray covered with glass.

"Here we've got what I'll call Exhibit B. Specimen of sand, stained with blood and"—he glanced uneasily towards the girls—"blood and—well, brain-tissue. We had to take 'em up, in case it rained. Other sand had been smoothed over 'em, so you didn't see 'em when you first looked. Also found not far from where Mr. Barlow was standing. The blood belongs to Group III, which they tell me's unusual. Mr. Morell's blood is Group III."

He replaced the tray.

When he produced the next object, it was one which sent a cold chill through the watchers. Perhaps this was caused by its whitish colour, its significant shape, its suggestion of death and mummification.

"Somebody," said Graham, "buried the cartridge-case and these blood-stained parts, and smoothed the sand out over them. What this fellow forgot was that it was a damp night. He left a clean, clear print of his right hand on the sand. We took a cast of it. This morning we got a specimen print of Mr. Barlow's right hand in sand before he knew what we were up to. The casts are the same. That print was made by Mr. Barlow's right hand."

"*Steady on, Jane!*" Fred said sharply.

A paralysis of horror lay on the group. It held them rigid. Though Fred's manner still seemed easy, the colour had left his face. White cast, black spot. White cast, black spot...

"You didn't," whispered Jane Tennant. "You didn't. For God's sake say you didn't."

The moaning voice attracted Mr. Justice Ireton's attention and annoyed him.

"Madam," he said, "you will pardon me if I ask you to leave this matter in my hands." He looked round again. "This does indeed appear to be serious. Have you, sir, any explanation of it?"

White cast, black spot. Black spot, clouding the mind and darkening it. Fred regarded the judge dully.

"Do *you* think I did it?" he asked, in a voice of heavy curiosity.

"I have not said what I think. But if you go on in this fashion, I fear you will leave me no choice. You either have an answer to this charge, or you have not. Will you produce that answer?"

"Not at the moment, no."

The judge looked thoughtful. "Perhaps you are wise. Yes, perhaps you are wise."

Fred continued to study him with the same heavy curiosity, breathing slowly. After this he turned to Graham.

"Good work, Inspector. Have you by any chance traced the revolver I used?"

"Not yet, sir; but with this other evidence we don't need to. We have a witness who testifies you usually carry a revolver in the right-hand side pocket of your motor car. And that's the whole story, to my way of thinking.

"This crime wasn't planned. That's to say, it was done on the spur of the moment. On Saturday night you started to drive in to Tawnish to get cigarettes, just like you told us. You were nearly to Lovers' Lane when you saw Mr. Morell walking along the road towards you. Now, you hated Mr. Morell. You can't deny that."

"No, I can't deny it."

"You had good reason for wanting him out of the way, as Miss Ireton can tell us. When you saw him walking towards you, on a lonely road where as a rule cars don't pass one every twenty minutes, I'm betting you had two thoughts. The first was: 'If Morell is going to see the judge, he's out of luck: because the judge is in London.' The second thought was: 'Cripes, I could kill him here; get rid of the bounder for good and all; and nobody'd ever be the wiser.'

"You're an impetuous sort of fellow, Frederick Barlow. That's how you do act: crash-bang, and think-about-it-afterwards. That's the way most murderers act, in my experience.

"You stopped your car and got out. He came up to you. You didn't even give the poor bloke a chance. You got the revolver out of the side pocket. He twigged what you were going to do; and turned round and tried to run to get away on the beach. There's a lamp-post a little way down from there, and you could see his outline. You shot him behind the ear just as he got to the opposite side of the road.

"Now, as a general rule, you'd still have been safe enough. It wasn't likely anybody would hear the shot, with the breakers thumping away; and, as I said, it's a lonely road. But by bad luck, when you went over to him, scared all of a sudden, and trying to decide what to do, along came Dr. Fellows.

"You had to think pretty fast. But nobody's ever accused you of being slow with your headpiece. You remembered that Black Jeff always dosses down in one of those model houses up Lovers' Lane. Jeff wears a butcher's coat that was once white but now's a kind of dirty grey, like Mr. Morell's suit. From behind, without the whiskers and the rest of it, this chap could be mistaken for Jeff in a bad light if you said it *was* Jeff. So you did, and the doctor went on.

"It was all right about Jeff. Everybody in town knew he'd been on a spree since Friday. Later, *he'd* never be able to remember where he'd been on Saturday night, or that he wasn't flopped down by the roadside like you said. But this body was different. If Mr. Morell's body's found here, or most anywhere in this district; if it isn't shown he was alive after you were seen bending over him; then Dr. Fellows is going to think back, and say to himself, 'Here!—What was—?' And you're for it. So you suddenly think to yourself: 'The judge's bungalow.'"

Fred spoke with a sick irony of cynicism.

"To throw suspicion on the judge, I suppose?"

"No! Not by a jugful! Because, you see, you thought he was in London and wouldn't get back until the last train. So *he'd* have an alibi for sure.

"You dumped Mr. Morell's body in your car, switched off the lights, backed round in Lovers' Lane, and drove to the bungalow. You had a look. It was all dark in front except for one little light in this room, which is exactly what you'd think a person would leave to light him home by in a dark neighbourhood. This room was empty.

"Your scheme, with the bullet and the chewing-gum you knew Mr. Morell carried, that was worked out in two minutes. I've heard you make some pretty smart use of spur-of-the-moment material in court, sir. Mr. Morell had got beach-sand on the front of his coat where he fell. You'd brushed most of that off, though (maybe you remember?) Bert Weems called our attention to some white sand still on the coat. And (you can't forget this, anyway) Mr. Morell's coat, when we saw it, still had patches of damp on the front of it."

It was Mr. Justice Ireton who spoke then.

"True," he remarked. "*I* recall it."

Graham snapped shut the clasps of the suitcase. "That's about all. You carried the body in; smeared his fingerprints on the 'phone and all over; used the handkerchief out of his breast-pocket (which we found there, remember?) for your own fingerprints; and played your trick. You'd just fired the shot, jumped down, and rolled the body close to the desk, when—"

"I heard someone coming, probably?" inquired Fred. His voice was still calm.

"Right. You heard the judge coming. You dropped the revolver and nipped out of the window. You *had* to leave that gun behind, to prove only one shot had been fired. But you were pretty sure we couldn't trace it to you; and we can't.

"There was only one other thing you had to do. You knew, after that 'phone-call, that the police would be coming in a brace of shakes, along the only road they could come. So back you went, left your car all smack and plain on the wrong side of the road with the lights on, and stopped Bert Weems with your story about Black Jeff, so you could fix that part of it in everybody's minds as clear as you'd fixed things in the telephone-girl's."

Graham concluded with bursting loudness. Then he got his breath after so much talking.

"Here's the proof," he added, tapping the suitcase.

"Your sole proof, Inspector? Pretty strong, I admit, but is that all you have against me?"

"No," said Graham in a flat voice. "That's why I wanted Miss Ireton to be here."

Constance had backed away until she was standing against the sideboard. She seemed to want to put as great a distance as possible between herself and Jane Tennant. Her face—pale, small-boned, delicate-featured—now seemed drawn as though with illness.

"M-me?" she stammered, and edged still further away.

"You see, sir," continued Graham, giving her a brief sympathetic smile before he turned to Mr. Justice Ireton, "we were never just satisfied with Miss Ireton's story. No. We still aren't. But we had it all wrong. Up to the time Dr. Fell explained about the extra bullet and the fake 'phone-call, we thought she was telling lies to protect *you*.

"But then, I thought to myself: '*How* is she protecting her father by what she testified?' She wasn't. She didn't. Nothing she said helped you very much; now did it? As a matter of fact, the only good solid thing she insisted on was…what was it? I'll tell you. It was that she saw Mr. Morell come along the road and go into this bungalow at twenty-five minutes past eight.

"Cripes, that was where I woke up! It wasn't her father she was protecting. It was Mr. Barlow."

Graham turned round and faced Constance. His manner was lowering and embarrassed; his face shone with a polished red rash under the bright lights; but his earnestness seemed to hypnotize her. He spoke not unkindly.

"Now, miss, here's how it is. We can prove that at twenty minutes past eight, two minutes or so after Mr. Morell must have been shot, you were in a telephone-box in Lovers' Lane only sixty feet away from the place. Even if we couldn't prove that, we should know you were telling us fibs. Mr. Morell was dead by eight twenty-five; and a man can't walk along a road with a bullet in his brain. You can't stick to that story unless you want to see real trouble.

"Miss, here's what I think. I think you saw Mr. Barlow shoot Mr. Morell."

He cleared his throat.

"Then I think you ran to that 'phone-box—sort of hysterical, like—and tried to ring up Miss Tennant. Probably to ask for a car to get you home. But you couldn't, so you went back to this bungalow. Hang it, miss, you *couldn't* have been as close as that, at that time, without seeing something or hearing the shot! Your lie about seeing Mr. Morell after he was dead proves you must have! The only question we had to think about was whether we ought to lock you up as accessory after the fact—"

"No!" cried Constance.

"I won't go on about that," said Graham, "because I don't want you to think I'm putting pressure on you. I'm not. All I say is: If you did see Mr. Barlow do that, it's your duty to tell me. You can't stick to what you've been saying. If you do, we're bound to keep on at you until we're satisfied, and you may find yourself in serious trouble."

Graham made a grimace which was evidently intended to be a sympathetic smile. He put out his hands.

"Now, come on, miss!" he urged persuasively. "Is what I've been saying true? Yes or no? Did you see anything? Did Mr. Barlow shoot Mr. Morell?"

Constance slowly raised her hands and pressed them against her face, either to hide it or to control emotion. They were delicate fingers, with red-painted nails, and ringless. While the seconds hammered on, clock-beats ticking into eternity, she stood rigid. Then her shoulders drooped. She let her hands fall and opened her eyes. The eyes seemed to be asking a question, asking for something which she hoped even now might be given to her.

"Yes," she said in a whisper. "He did it."

"Ah!" said Graham, and expelled his breath.

Mr. Justice Ireton's cigar had long ago gone out. He picked it up from the edge of the ashtray on the chess table, and lit it again.

Jane Tennant uttered a moaning cry, a kind of whimper. The sheer incredulousness of her look had never faded. She kept shaking her head from side to side, violently, but not speaking.

Nor did Dr. Fell speak.

Fred Barlow slapped his knees as though with decision, and got up from the arm of the sofa. He walked across to Jane. Her face, which was as cold as marble, he took between his hands; and he kissed her.

"Don't worry," he said with clear reassurance. "I'll beat them. Their times are all wrong, for one thing. But—but the circumstantial evidence..."

He rubbed his hands across his forehead, as though in desperation. He glanced at Mr. Justice Ireton, but the judge's face was stony.

"All right, Inspector," he concluded, lifting his shoulders, "I'll go quietly."

CHAPTER XX

ON THE EVENING OF THE DAY FOLLOWING FREDERICK Barlow's detention, Tuesday, April thirtieth—which is May Day eve, when evil spirits are said to walk—Mr. Justice Ireton sat in the living-room of his bungalow, playing chess with Dr. Gideon Fell.

An electric heater burned beside their table, for the evening was stormy. The sea wind came at the windows with a pounce and slap; the sea charged the beach as an army might charge it; the night outside was white-flecked and stung with spray.

But the heater burned warmly. The lights were snug. The chess pieces, red and white, gleamed in crooked array on their board. Neither the judge nor Dr. Fell had spoken for some time. Both contemplated the board.

Dr. Fell cleared his throat.

"Sir," he asked, without looking up, "have you spent a pleasant day?"

"Eh?"

"I said: Have you spent a pleasant day?"

"Not particularly," replied the judge, making his move at last.

"I refer," said Dr. Fell, moving in reply, "to the supposition that this day cannot have been very pleasant for your daughter. She is fond of Frederick Barlow. Yet in the interests of justice she will be forced to go into the witness-box and send him to death. Still, there is the philosophical side. As you said yourself, nothing in this world is of less importance than human relationships."

Again they were silent, studying the board.

"Then there is young Barlow himself," pursued Dr. Fell. "A decent lad, when all is said and done. He had a great future before him. Not any longer. Even if he is acquitted of this charge (which I consider unlikely), he will be ruined. He stood by you at a difficult time. You must feel rather friendly towards him yourself. But, as you say, nothing in this world is of less importance than human relationships."

Mr. Justice Ireton frowned at the board, considering it. He made his move after more deliberation.

"Incidentally," resumed Dr. Fell, moving in reply, "it will break the heart of a girl named Jane Tennant. Perhaps you noticed her face, when they took her away yesterday? But, then!—you hardly know her. And in any case, as you say, nothing in this world..."

Mr. Justice Ireton glanced up briefly, behind his big spectacles, before he resumed his scrutiny of the board.

"What sort of chess are you playing?" he complained, displeased with the position he saw there.

"It is a little development of my own," said Dr. Fell.

"So?"

"Yes. You would probably call it the cat-and-mouse gambit. It consists of letting your opponent think he's perfectly safe, winning hands down: and then catching him in a corner."

"You think you can win with *that* position?"

"I can try. What do you think of Graham's case against Barlow?"

The judge frowned.

"A strong case," he conceded, with his eyes on the board. "Not a perfect case. But a satisfying case."

He made his move.

"Yes, isn't it?" agreed Dr. Fell, striking his fist on the arm of the chair with subdued but hearty enthusiasm. "That's just the word for it. Rounded, complete, with few if any loose ends. Satisfying! Such cases often are. It is an explanation which covers all or most of the facts. It is an explanation which is rather convincing. What a pity that it isn't the true explanation!"

As he bent forward to move a piece in turn, Dr. Fell looked up and added:

"For of course you and I know that it was really you who shot Morell."

Outside, the hard gusts drove across sand, masked in spray. The distant thunder of breakers seemed to make the stuffed moose's head vibrate against the wall. Mr. Justice Ireton stretched out a hand towards the electric heater; still he did not look up, but his lips tightened.

"Your move," he said.

"You have no comment to make?"

"Only that you would have to prove it."

"Exactly!" agreed Dr. Fell, with a sort of pounce, and the same rich enthusiasm. "And I can't prove it! That is the curious beauty of it. The truth is too incredible. Nobody would believe me. If you are uneasy about your own safety, at least in this world, put the thought out of your mind. Your Roman stoicism has its reward. You committed a murder. You are letting a friend of yours swing for it. You cannot be convicted. I congratulate you."

The thin lips tightened still more.

"Your move," repeated the judge patiently. But after the other had made it he added: "And what makes you believe I killed Mr. Morell?"

"My dear sir, I was sure of it as soon as I heard about the revolver you stole from Sir Charles Hawley."

"Indeed."

"Yes. But there again you are protected. You are protected by the word of an eminent man who dares not betray you, and against whom my word would weigh no more than *that*." He snapped his fingers. "Just as you are protected by your daughter, who loves you. Who saw you commit the murder. But who is compelled to say it was Barlow, because otherwise she would have to admit it was you. Again I congratulate you. Did you sleep well last night?"

"*God—damn you!*" said Horace Ireton in two gasps, and brought down his fist on the table with a crash that jarred the chess pieces.

Dr. Fell set about quietly restoring the shaken chessmen to their proper squares.

"Be good enough," said the judge, after a pause, "to tell me what you know, or think you know."

"You are interested?"

"I am waiting."

Dr. Fell leaned back, and sat listening as though to the storm.

"There was a man," he said, "placed in the seats of the mighty, who had let his position go to his head. His sin (shall we say?) was not that he judged hardly or harshly. His sin was that he began to think himself infallible: that he could not make a mistake in judging men.

"But he could and he did.

"This man, to protect his daughter, resolved to commit murder. But he was a jurist. He had seen more murderers than there are lines in the palm of his hand. He had seen murderers clever, murderers stupid, murderers cowardly, murderers brave. And he knew that there is no such thing as a perfect crime.

"He knew that what defeats the murderer is not the imperfection of his plans or the cleverness of the police. What defeats the murderer is accident: the dozens of little unforeseen chances which lurk every step of the way. Somebody looks out of a window at the wrong time. Somebody notices a gold tooth, or remembers a song. So this man knew that the best crime is the simplest: that is, the one which presents fewest opportunities both to chance and to the police.

"Procure a revolver from a source which cannot be traced to you. Waylay your victim where nobody sees you. Shoot him, and walk away. They may suspect you. They may ask awkward questions. But they can never prove anything.

"So this man, Horace Ireton, told Anthony Morell to come to his house by the coast road—and told him when to come.

On the following day he went to London, stole a fully loaded gun from a source we guess, and returned to his bungalow.

"At some minutes past eight o'clock he put on a pair of gloves, put the revolver in his pocket, and left his house. He walked by the back path across the meadows—where? To Lovers' Lane, of course. That is the only side road joining the main road between here and Tawnish. It has high banks in whose shadow he can wait unseen until the victim approaches. Such a choice was inevitable.

"At about eighteen minutes past eight, Morell came along. Horace Ireton wasted no time or words. He stepped out of the lane and took the gun from his pocket. Morell saw him by the street-lamp, and knew. Morell turned; he began to run diagonally across the road, away and towards the sands. Horace Ireton shot him. Morell took a step more and fell. The murderer went to him as he lay on the edge of the sand, dropped the pistol beside him, turned, and went away quietly the way he had come.

"Meanwhile, the same old, old chance had cropped up again: that unforeseen witness. Constance Ireton had decided to see her father that night. Her car ran out of petrol. She walked to the bungalow, and found nobody there. She suddenly remembered that it was Saturday; that he must be in London. So she decided to walk the short distance to Tawnish, and get a bus there.

"And she saw the thing done.

"When she saw her father walk away afterwards, she was (I think) frantic. She could not and would not approach Morell, whom she then believed to deserve what had been given him. Her legs would hardly hold her. She wanted *help*, as always. Remembering the telephone-box, she ran up the lane and attempted to 'phone Taunton.

"Therefore she did not see the fact which has turned this whole affair into a nightmare."

Dr. Fell paused.

Mr. Justice Ireton sat motionless, his hands folded over his stomach, while the storm rattled.

"And what was it she failed to see?" he inquired.

"That Morell was not dead," said Dr. Fell.

Mr. Justice Ireton closed his eyes. A spasm went over his face, but it was a spasm of realization, a shock of revelation. He opened his eyes, and said:

"You ask me to believe that a man with a bullet in his brain was not yet dead?"

"Didn't I tell you it was incredible?" demanded Dr. Fell, with a sort of eagerness. "Didn't I say nobody would believe it?" His tone changed. "The thing is, of course, a commonplace of medical jurisprudence. John Wilkes Booth, the assassin of President Lincoln, moved and talked for some time with much the same sort of injury before he died. Gross quotes the case of a man who, after getting four and a half inches of steel through his brain, even recovered afterwards. Taylor quotes several such instances; of which the most interesting, medically speaking—"

"You may spare me your authorities, if you will be good enough to explain."

"Morell," said Dr. Fell simply, "wasn't dead yet. He was as good as dead; but he didn't know it. For the moment, he was most viciously and viperishly alive."

"Ah!"

"What has happened to Anthony Morell, *né* Morelli? As his stunned wits start to work again, as he crawls and staggers up from that sand, what does he realize has happened?

"Well, that what happened before has happened once again. He has tried smoothly to work a game on somebody, and has got his answer in the form of a revolver bullet. Mr. Justice Ireton—the holy, the mighty, the man Morell hates—has tried to shoot him dead. But, if he tells the police this, will he be believed? No. Even less than in the Lee case, where the mighty ones of this world clubbed together to ridicule and discredit him. But this time they are not going to get away with it. This time, by all his Sicilian gods, he will have it his own way."

Dr. Fell paused.

"My dear sir," he went on, settling back more comfortably in the chair and speaking with an air of wonder, "should you say for one moment that all this hocus-pocus with telephones and chewing-gum sounds like Fred Barlow? Should you, as a jurist, say it was good psychology? I say no. I say there is only one person it does sound like. It sounds like Morell."

Mr. Justice Ireton did not comment.

"His intention, in your view," the judge said, "being—?"

"To provide unanswerable proof, when he later comes to accuse you, that *you* shot him."

"Ah!"

"Someone once described Morell to me as 'a sort of crude Borgia.' His lawyer declares that he would work out the most elaborate and Machiavellian schemes of revenge if he thought someone had done him a slight or an injury. Well, what you did to him might mildly be described as an injury. You agree?"

"Go on."

"And here is his chance. He *must* reach that bungalow before you, at your slow walk, get there. He picks up the revolver, sees what calibre it is, and puts it in his pocket. He hurries straight along the main road. Sir, he did reach the place at eight twenty-five after all. Had your daughter been at the gate, she *would* have seen him, chewing-gum and looking like fire, go in to get his own back at last.

"It was Morell who put through that fake call and fired the second shot. But when he called for help, he needed it. That was the end. He could go no further, once that gum masked the bullet-hole. The revolver, which he had wrapped in his handkerchief to avoid his own fingerprints, fell from his hand. The chair upset beneath him. And he fell dead beside the wreck of the telephone."

Dr. Fell drew a long breath.

"I don't wonder you were surprised," he added, "when you came in from the kitchen and found him there. Is 'surprised' quite the right word, even?"

Mr. Justice Ireton did not say whether it was the right word. But his mouth worked slightly.

"I don't wonder," pursued Dr. Fell, "that you picked up the revolver, and were perhaps a little surprised—a little—to find only one bullet still gone. I don't wonder you sat down, dumbly, and tried to think. Most murderers would be more upset than you if their carefully placed victims came home."

"You assume much," said the judge.

"And your daughter, too," said Dr. Fell, "was considerably surprised. She finished her futile efforts at the 'phone; and returned by the back path because she could not, would not, pass Morell's body again. She was in time (I indulge my fancy here) to hear the second shot from a distance. She saw nobody in the kitchen. She circled the house, looked in at the front, and saw you.

"This also provided her with the realistic detail, later put into her story, about the central lights being turned on. Only the little lamp was burning when she first looked in here on her way past. All the lights were on later.

"Her tale about Morell's arrival at eight twenty-five was, of course, an attempt to shield you by turning attention away from Lovers' Lane and the real time of the murder. You were in trouble when she told it. But you would have been in a damned sight worse trouble had we known you really did kill Morell at an earlier place and time. Unfortunately, the astute Inspector Graham interpreted it as applying to Barlow. It is a good thing for you. But it will hang an innocent man."

Mr. Justice Ireton removed his spectacles, and began to swing them back and forth.

"The evidence against Fred Barlow—"

"Oh, my dear sir!" protested Dr. Fell dismally.

"You do not call it evidence?"

"Barlow," said Dr. Fell, "was driving in to Tawnish. With all due respect to the clock in the car belonging to Dr. Fellows, whose name is associated with mine as such a sinister omen, I submit that his statement is tosh and eyewash. I submit that his time is all wrong. Barlow thinks so himself. I submit that the time was nearer eight-thirty than eight-twenty.

"Morell had gone long before. Black Jeff, either by chance or still trying to trace the source of a revolver shot he had heard, came out of his haunt in Lovers' Lane and fell smack in front of the car. Barlow thought he had run over the man.

"He carried Jeff to the other side of the road. Dr. Fellows passed. Barlow, to see how badly Jeff was hurt, got an electric torch from his car and returned to the place where he thought he had left his victim. But Jeff had crawled away.

"Barlow (as he told us, once) thought he must have mistaken the spot where he had put Jeff down. He walked all along the bank, flashing his light. And presently he saw..."

"Yes?" inquired the judge.

"He saw blood," said Dr. Fell. "And brain-tissue."

Mr. Justice Ireton put a hand over his eyes.

"Well, what did the lad naturally think?" asked Dr. Fell. "What would *you* have thought? Not you, perhaps, since you would no doubt preserve a more stoical attitude than most of us. But the average person?"

"I—!"

"He thought he had done for Black Jeff. So he smoothed over the traces. That's all. I doubt if he ever even noticed that tiny brass cartridge-case, which was smoothed over with the rest of it.

"The thing haunted him. If you talk to Miss Tennant (as I did, last night) you will hear what Barlow once said: that he knew, from positive evidence, that he had badly hurt Black Jeff. That's the evidence. It is the same evidence Graham will use to prove he killed Morell. I am aware that the matter, personally, is of no interest to you. You were very severe with Barlow last night, I remember, for not being able to explain it."

"I—"

"No one, as you once said to me, has ever accused you of

being a hypocrite or a stuffed shirt. Still, the matter is surely of some academic interest to you. Are your beliefs so unshaken, sir? Do you still maintain, from your private knowledge, that circumstances can never hang an innocent man?"

"I tell you—"

"Then there is your daughter," continued Dr. Fell, surveying the matter dispassionately. "The ordeal in court will not be pleasant for her. She now has some three months in which to look forward to it. She is faced with the choice of saving Barlow or of saving you. She does not love Barlow, or the result might be different. She has for him only an adolescent liking based on long acquaintanceship. She will, of course, save her father. It is a necessary choice. But it is a cruel choice."

Again Mr. Justice Ireton struck the table, making the chessmen jump.

"Stop this," he said. "Stop these cat-and-mouse tactics. I won't have it, do you hear?" His voice rose pettishly. "Do you think I like doing what I've had to do? Do you think I'm not human?"

Dr. Fell considered.

"'I have not said what I think,'" he replied in the voice of one who quotes, "'But if you go on in this fashion, I fear you will leave me no choice. You either have an answer to these charges, or you have not. Will you produce that answer?'"

Mr. Justice Ireton put down his spectacles on the table. He sat back, shading his eyes with his hand. He breathed thinly, like a man facing exertion after a sedentary life.

"God help me," he said, "I cannot go on with this."

But when he removed his hand from shading his eyes, his face was smoothed-out, pale, and calm again. With an effort he got to his feet and walked across to the desk. From the upper drawer he took a long envelope, and returned to the table again. He did not sit down.

"A while ago, Doctor, you asked me whether I had spent a pleasant day. I did not spend it pleasantly. But I spent it profitably. I spent it in writing a confession."

From the envelope he took several sheets of notepaper covered with his fine, neat handwriting. He replaced it, and tossed the envelope across to Dr. Fell.

"It covers, I think, such points as will effect the boy's release. I must ask, however, that you do not deliver it to Inspector Graham for twenty-four hours. By that time I have every reasonable hope of being dead. It will be difficult, under the circumstances, to make my death appear an accident. But my life is insured for a large sum, which will take care of Constance; and I trust I shall be able to manage suicide more expertly than I appear to have managed murder. There is your confession. Pick it up, please."

He watched while Dr. Fell did so. Then the blood rushed into his face.

"Now that I have made the *amende honorable*," he added in a cold, steady voice, "shall I tell you what I think?"

"Yes?"

"I do not think," said Mr. Justice Ireton, "that Fred Barlow is under arrest at all."

"Indeed," said Dr. Fell.

"I have read all of today's newspapers. Not a word appears in any of them about this rather sensational capture."

"So."

"I think that this whole arrest is a trick, deliberately devised and staged between you and Graham, in order to extort a confession from me. It struck me once or twice yesterday that Graham's acting was nervous. I think that the boy is being 'detained' while you are sent to apply torture of a refined and effective sort.

"But I dare not take the risk. I dare not call your bluff. I cannot trust my judgment any longer. It is just possible Graham does mean what he says. It is just possible he will bring that boy to trial, and ruin him if he does not convict him.

"On your own part in this, Gideon Fell, I pass no comment. You can cry checkmate. You can crack the whip. You wanted to beat me at my own game; and, if it is any source of satisfaction to you, you have done so." His voice broke. "Now take your damned confession, and go."

Thinly the storm whistled round the house. But Dr. Fell did not move.

He sat turning the envelope over in his hands, sunk in dim and obscure meditation. He hardly seemed to hear what the judge was saying. He took the sheets of paper from the envelope, and slowly read them through, wheezing gently as he did so. Then he folded them up with equal slowness, tore them in three pieces, and threw the pieces on the table.

"No," he said. "*You* win."

"Pardon?"

"You're quite right," assented Dr. Fell, heavily and wearily. "Graham no more believes Barlow is guilty than I do. He's known it was you all along. But you were just a little too legally nimble for us; so we had to think of another way. The only other person who knows about this now is Miss Tennant. I couldn't refrain from telling her last night, as I can't refrain from telling you now. I have only one other thing to say to you: go free."

There was a pause.

"Explain that extraordinary statement."

"I said: go free," repeated Dr. Fell, waving his hand rather testily. "Don't expect me to apologize to you as well. I shall tell Graham that it didn't work, that's all."

"But—"

"There will be a flaming scandal, of course. You will have to resign from the bench. But they can't touch you now that there's so infernally much confusion as to what *did* happen."

The judge sat down heavily, making the table quiver.

"You quite understand what you are saying, Doctor? You mean this?"

"Yes."

"Doctor," observed Mr. Justice Ireton abruptly, "I do not know what to say."

"There is nothing to say. I can inform you, though, that your plans for your daughter will not materialize. She will not marry Fred Barlow. Barlow, I am happy to say, will marry Jane Tennant: who will manage him admirably while he thinks he is managing her. Your daughter is now interested in some young man named Hugo, about whom I know nothing except that he seems likely to meet an early demise in the swimming-pool. For the rest, you have come well out of this. So go your ways, and don't be so ruddy cocksure about your judgment in the future."

While Mr. Justice Ireton shaded his eyes with his hand, Dr. Fell dropped the pieces of the confession into the ashtray. He struck a match to them. The flames curled up as the paper caught fire, and were reflected in the eyes of the moose's head on the wall. Both men sat silent, watching truth burn.

If you've enjoyed *The Seat of the Scornful*,
you won't want to miss

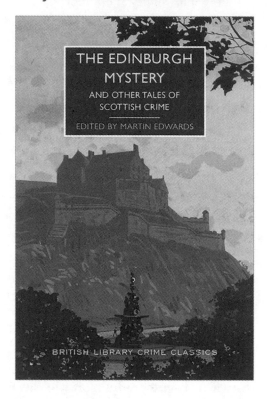

the most recent BRITISH LIBRARY CRIME CLASSIC
published by Poisoned Pen Press,
an imprint of Sourcebooks.

poisonedpenpress.com

Don't miss these favorite British Library Crime Classics available from Poisoned Pen Press!

Mysteries written during the Golden Age of Detective Fiction, beloved by readers and reviewers

Antidote to Venom
by Freeman Wills Crofts

Bats in the Belfry
by E. C. R. Lorac

Blood on the Tracks:
Railway Mysteries
edited by Martin Edwards

Calamity in Kent
by John Rowland

Christmas Card Crime
and Other Stories
edited by Martin Edwards

Cornish Coast Murder
by John Bude

Continental Crimes
edited by Martin Edwards

Crimson Snow: Winter Mysteries
edited by Martin Edwards

Death in the Tunnel
by Miles Burton

Death of a Busybody
by George Bellairs

Death on the Riviera
by John Bude

Fell Murder
by E. C. R. Lorac

Incredible Crime
by Lois Austen-Leigh

Miraculous Mysteries
edited by Martin Edwards

Murder at the Manor
edited by Martin Edwards

Murder in the Museum
by John Rowland

Murder of a Lady
by Anthony Wynne

Praise for the
British Library Crime Classics

"Carr is at the top of his game in this taut whodunit... The British Library Crime Classics series has unearthed another worthy golden age puzzle."

—*Publishers Weekly*, STARRED Review, for *The Lost Gallows*

"A wonderful rediscovery."
—*Booklist*, STARRED Review, for *The Sussex Downs Murder*

"First-rate mystery and an engrossing view into a vanished world."

—*Booklist*, STARRED Review, for *Death of an Airman*

"A cunningly concocted locked-room mystery, a staple of Golden Age detective fiction."

—*Booklist*, STARRED Review, for *Murder of a Lady*

"The book is both utterly of its time and utterly ahead of it."
—*New York Times Book Review* for *The Notting Hill Mystery*

"As with the best of such compilations, readers of classic mysteries will relish discovering unfamiliar authors, along with old favorites such as Arthur Conan Doyle and G.K. Chesterton."
—*Publishers Weekly*, STARRED Review, for *Continental Crimes*

"In this imaginative anthology, Edwards—president of Britain's Detection Club—has gathered together overlooked criminous gems."

—*Washington Post* for *Crimson Snow*

"The degree of suspense Crofts achieves by showing the growing obsession and planning is worthy of Hitchcock. Another first-rate reissue from the British Library Crime Classics series."

—*Booklist*, STARRED Review, for *The 12.30 from Croydon*

"Not only is this a first-rate puzzler, but Crofts's outrage over the financial firm's betrayal of the public trust should resonate with today's readers."

—*Booklist,* STARRED Review, for *Mystery in the Channel*

"This reissue exemplifies the mission of the British Library Crime Classics series in making an outstanding and original mystery accessible to a modern audience."

—*Publishers Weekly*, STARRED Review, for *Excellent Intentions*

"A book to delight every puzzle-suspense enthusiast."

—*New York Times* for *The Colour of Murder*

"Edwards's outstanding third winter-themed anthology showcases 11 uniformly clever and entertaining stories, mostly from lesser known authors, providing further evidence of the editor's expertise… This entry in the British Library Crime Classics series will be a welcome holiday gift for fans of the golden age of detection."

—*Publishers Weekly,* STARRED Review, for
The Christmas Card Crime and Other Stories

poisonedpenpress.com